More books in the **Lone Wolf Howls** series
THE LOST TEMPLE OF TOTEC: BOOK ONE
THE ONE-EYED MULE SKINNER: BOOK TWO
THE BLACK PEARL TREASURE: BOOK THREE
THE HIDDEN FORTRESS: BOOK FOUR

ALSO BY ERIC T KNIGHT
IMMORTALITY AND CHAOS
(epic fantasy series)
Wreckers Gate: Book One
Landsend Plateau: Book Two
Guardians Watch: Book Three
Hunger's Reach: Book Four
Oblivion's Grasp: Book Five

CHAOS AND RETRIBUTION
(sequel to Immortality and Chaos)
Stone Bound: Book One
Sky Touched: Book Two
Sea Born: Book Three
Chaos Trapped: Book Four
Shadow Hunted: Book Five
Power Forged: Book Six

THE ACTION THRILLER
WATCHING THE END OF THE WORLD

Follow me at
er
All books ava

D1468839

ACE LONE WOLF
and the
Secrets of Machu Picchu
by
Eric T Knight

Chapter 1

It's a normal day in San Francisco. By that I mean it's cold and gray and rainy. It's been cold and gray and rainy every single day since I got here. Why do people live here? Is it always like this, or did I come at a bad time?

I miss the sun. I can't remember the last time I saw it. For a while this afternoon there was a glowing spot in the sky, but it's gone now. Night is coming on fast.

Rain is running off the brim of my hat and dripping down my back. I've got puddles in my boots. Coyote hates it too. He's got his ears back, and he's whipping his tail around like he does when he's in a really bad mood. I better watch my step when I get off. He's likely to take a chunk out of my shoulder. Coyote is ornery that way.

Hunkered down in my duster like I am, I don't notice the man waving his arms at me. He has to yell to get my attention.

"Hey, you're Ace Lone Wolf, aren't you?"

I don't look at him. Whatever he wants, I'm not interested. Ever since I took a train up here from the Arizona Territory to talk to that newspaper man, I've had people recognizing me. I don't much like that. Being noticed isn't a healthy thing, in my experience. You get noticed too much, sooner or later someone decides to take a shot at you.

I should have told the newspaper man no. I said yes because it sounded like easy money. Fifty dollars and a train ticket to get my picture taken and answer some questions? Who'd say no to that? I'd have to spend almost two months punching cows to make that much.

I also took it because I needed to get out of Arizona for a bit. Things had gotten a little hot down there on account of a misunderstanding I had with the governor's son. And by misunderstanding, I mean Coyote took a bite out of his ear. When he thought to reply with hot lead, I had no choice but to shoot him. It was only in the foot, but his pa didn't feel all that

1

charitable afterwards. I barely got out of Phoenix ahead of two deputies and a hanging rope.

Anyhow, the newspaper man asked a whole lot of questions, mostly about the gunfights I've been in. He wanted to know if it was true I was in the gunfight at the OK Corral with Doc Holliday and the Earps. I told him it was. Then he wanted to know if it was true I faced Wes Hardin and Killin' Jim by myself.

About then the whole thing started to make me a mite antsy. See, the thing about making a name for yourself as a gunslick, is that pretty soon every two-bit rooster with a pistol and dreams of glory wants a piece of you. I don't need that particular brand of trouble any more than I need another hole in my head. Which is what I'd end up with, sooner or later.

But I got real jumpy when he asked if it was true I'm the grandson of the famous Apache chief Cochise. That's not a flag I want to go waving about. My clan has been living free in the Sierra Madre Mountains in northern Mexico for twenty years or so. Except for a handful of *Netdahe* like Geronimo, we're pretty much the only Apaches not on a reservation these days. Part of the reason we've been able to pull it off is we keep our heads down. We don't bother anyone, and they don't bother us.

I told the newspaper man I'm half-Apache—my mother is Apache, my father a shiftless gambler—but I said that stuff about Cochise isn't true.

Which didn't stop him from printing it.

Ever since that story came out it's given me nothing but trouble. I wish I'd never done it.

So when the man calls out to me, I pull my hat down lower and keep on going. But he isn't giving up that easy.

He comes splashing out into the street and peers up at me. He's got little round glasses and the rain is streaking them, but he doesn't seem to care.

"It *is* you. I recognize you from your picture."

I rein Coyote to a stop. "And what if it is? What do you want?" The rain has me cranky. I swear, if he wants me to show him how fast I can draw, I'm going to point my gun at him. That will show him.

"I've got something for you." He grins at me. He's got front teeth like a beaver.

2

My right hand drifts closer to the butt of my gun, and I look him over suspiciously. But he's got no gun I can see, and he seems harmless enough.

"Wait here," he says, and takes off at a trot.

He disappears inside. I look at the sign and see that the building is a post office. I've never been in a post office before.

Real quick he's back outside. He holds up a long envelope. "It's not often we get mail from Peru. Or ever."

I take it from him. I got to admit I'm curious now. No one I know writes letters. I glance at it. It's got my name on it all right, and San Francisco, but nothing else. I tuck it into my saddlebag before it melts in the rain.

"Is it true that Cochise is your grandpa?" he asks.

"No." I twitch the reins and Coyote starts walking again. But the little guy doesn't give up that easy. He trots along by my knee.

"Is it true you faced Wes Hardin and Killin' Jim by yourself?"

"I don't recall," I say. "It was some time ago." I kind of push him away with my foot. I don't actually kick him, even if I want to.

Then he says something I never expected.

"Can I get your autograph, mister?"

I look down at him. "What?"

"Your autograph."

"I don't know what that is."

"Your signature. On a piece of paper."

I stare at him in disbelief. "Why ever would you want that?"

"To keep. Because you're famous."

He's serious. "You're addled," I tell him.

"Please."

Well, shoot. How can I say no? He said please and everything. What can it hurt? "All right."

"You'll have to come inside." He gestures at the sky. "The rain and all, right?"

There's a giant mud puddle in front of the post office that I don't fancy slogging through, so I ride Coyote over to the hitching post in front of the mercantile next door.

I don't tie Coyote to the hitching post. For one thing, it wouldn't make any difference. If Coyote decides to leave, no knot is going to stop him. For another, Coyote is free to leave whenever he wants. He stays with me as long as he wants to. I don't own him.

I follow the man along the boardwalk to the post office, and we go inside. He scurries around behind the counter and rummages through a drawer. He comes up with pencil and a little notebook and sets them on the counter. He opens the notebook to a blank page.

I pick up the pencil and look at him. "That's all I do, just write my name?"

"That's all," he says. Then he gets a sheepish look. "You could write, 'To my good friend Ralph'. If you want to."

"You're Ralph?"

"Yep."

"I don't know you."

He shrugs. "Won't anyone know that."

He's got a point there. I write the words and scrawl my moniker at the end. My writing is purely awful. It looks like someone dunked a chicken's feet in ink and let it run wild on the paper. As I slide the notebook back to him, I notice something.

"You have others in here."

"That I do." He clutches the notebook to his chest and smiles proudly. "I've met a lot of famous gunfighters. Wild Bill Hickok. Clay Allison. Bat Masterson. Wyatt Earp."

"Hold on. Did you say Wyatt Earp?"

"I did."

I try to imagine Wyatt agreeing to sign his little notebook and can't. He doesn't seem the type to tolerate foolishness. "How'd you wrangle that?" I ask him. "Wyatt's not the easiest feller."

"It was his brother Morgan that spoke up for me."

I flip my collar up and head out the door. It's raining even harder. I pull my hat down tighter. Ralph waves at me through the window. I lift a hand and hurry away. I have to get out of this rain.

What with the rain, and me being in a hurry and all, I don't see the two men who step out of the alley until it's too late.

Chapter 2

They're wearing ponchos and wide-brimmed straw hats, pulled down low. I can't see much of their faces. I sure enough see the knives they're flashing though. The taller one holds his right up under my nose. It's about as long as his forearm.

"The map," he says in a rough voice. "Give us the map." He's got an accent I can't quite place. He sounds kind of Mexican, but different. He's fairly dark skinned, with a bushy black mustache.

"Mister, I don't know what you're talking about. But if you don't get that pig sticker out of my face, we're going to have trouble." While I'm talking, I'm trying to figure how to get to my guns. I wear a pair of them, matching Colt .45 Peacemakers, and I'm fairly handy with them.

But they're under my duster, and it's buttoned up tight. And under the duster is my other coat. It could take me the rest of the day to dig them out.

"You lie," he says. "I see you come out of the post office. Give it to me or I cut you."

Now it's starting to make sense. He's talking about the letter. He and his partner must have just gotten here, or they'd have seen me put it in my saddlebag.

I don't want any trouble. I sure don't want a map that people are all hot to stab me for. If he was to ask me all friendly-like, I probably would give him the durned thing.

But here's the thing. I don't take kindly to people threatening me. Now I've got my dander up. Which means I'm not feeling very friendly anymore.

I figure talking isn't going to get us over this hill. It's time to do something.

I take a step forward. He's not expecting that. After all, he's got a knife. He expects me to move away from the knife, not closer.

I grab his wrist and give it a twist. He yelps and drops the knife.

I hammer him twice in the face real quick and turn to his partner.

He slashes at my ribs. I'm not fast enough to dodge his attack. The knife hits home.

But I don't feel a thing. The knife doesn't make it through the coats I'm wearing. It gets snagged in the duster.

I bring my elbow around and crack his jaw for him. A bloody tooth flies out.

I shift my weight to my back foot and kick him. It's a good, solid kick, and it catches him square. He falls off the boardwalk into that big mud puddle.

Back to the one with the mustache. He's got his knife back and he's charging at me, stabbing overhand as he comes.

I step aside. The knife hisses by my face. He's off balance now, so it's easy to grab him, turn, and let his own momentum carry him off the boardwalk to join his partner in the mud puddle.

I touch my hat. "Good day, gentlemen." I start to walk away.

I have only the briefest glimpse of motion out of the corner of my eye. I raise my arm and start to turn, but it's already too late.

Something hard hits me behind the ear. Everything goes black.

Chapter 3

I wake up in a whole world of hurt. It feels like someone's beating on my head with a hammer. From the inside. My eyes don't want to focus. I blink a few times, trying to sort out what's happened.

The first thing I realize is I'm wet. I'm lying on the ground. Water is soaking in everywhere. There's rain falling on my face.

I sure am tired of the rain.

Motion, and then a face appears in my vision. It's the man with the mustache. He's bleeding from a cut on his cheek, and he's covered in mud. He looks downright riled. Behind him are the other two, giving me their best rattlesnake looks.

"I gave you a chance," he says, waving his knife in front of my face. "This could have been easy, but you made it hard. Now you will be sorry."

"Looking at your face is making me sorry," I say.

That earns me a good hard slap that sends stars across my vision. I really should learn to think before I talk.

"The map. Give it to me." He shows his teeth when he talks, like he's thinking about biting me. They don't look so good, mostly brown and yellow.

"What do you want a map for? Are you lost? I'd be happy to—"

I don't finish before he gives me another wallop. Clearly he isn't the talkative sort.

"I'm getting tired of that," I tell him.

"Give me the map or I cut your throat," he hisses, pressing the blade to my throat.

"I won't be able to tell you where it is if you do that."

His expression says he hadn't thought of that.

"I tell you what," I say. "You let me up. We'll go to a nice, dry saloon and palaver. Could be I'll remember better if I have a beer in my hand." While I'm talking, I'm feeling around for my guns. With any luck my attackers missed one of them.

7

"Looking for these?" one of the others says, holding up my gun belt.

"I am. I guess I dropped them. You mind handing them over?"

"Enough!" the one holding the knife snaps. "No more warnings. Give me the map."

"I told you, I don't have any maps today. Check back tomorrow. Maybe I'll have one then."

"Now I cut pieces off you," he says. "You will talk then."

He barks an order at the other two. One stands on my arms. The other gets hold of my legs. The leader takes hold of my right hand, pulls my trigger finger out and presses his knife up to it. "Last chance. Give me the map or I cut it off."

I'm running out of time. But I'm not out of options. I still have one more card to play.

I'm betting that I'm in the alley between the post office and the mercantile. I better be, or this isn't going to work. But I don't think they carried me very far after knocking me out. Too much chance of someone seeing them. I'm thinking they dragged me back far enough where passersby wouldn't see me.

Time to get a little help.

I whistle.

"Why are you whistling?" the leader asks, frowning.

"Wait for it," I tell him.

There's a long moment where nothing happens, and I get a sick feeling in my gut. Maybe he's not coming. He's been pretty peevish lately. He doesn't like it here in the city.

"Coyote!" I yell.

And there it comes, the sound I've been waiting for.

The thunder of hooves.

"You haven't met my friend," I tell the man. "He's a lot meaner than I am."

The men turn, peering through the rain. The one holding my legs stands up and takes a couple steps toward the sound.

Coyote comes bursting out of the gloom, hooves pounding, throwing mud everywhere.

He's a beautiful sight.

The one standing holds up his knife. Coyote simply runs over him. There's a crack of bone breaking, and he goes flying, smacking into the wall and slumping to the ground.

The other two are yelling. The one kneeling on my arm lunges for my pistols, which are lying on the ground. Coyote stomps on his hand. More bones break. He squalls and falls back, clutching his wounded hand to his chest.

The leader's got a little more brains than the other two. Not much, or he'd be running, but a little more. He's already drawing his pistol as he stands. He draws bead on Coyote.

But now there's no one holding me. I'm not going to lie here and watch my horse get shot.

I throw myself at his legs. His shot goes wild, whining down the alley.

Coyote rears up. Hooves flash, and the man folds up and drops like a wet sack.

I climb to my feet and retrieve my gun belt. Both guns are covered in mud. They're going to need a good cleaning.

Coyote lowers his head and sniffs the leader. He sneezes, blowing horse snot all over the man's face. Then he gives me a sideways look. I know that look.

"Yeah, I know. You saved my bacon again. There's no need to rub it in."

The other two get to their feet and run away. I consider chasing them. I'd sure like some answers. But I'm cold and wet and my head hurts something awful.

I check the leader. He's out cold. I'm not getting any answers out of him.

"Let's get out of here," I say to Coyote. "We don't want to be here if the law starts sniffing around." There's no predicting how the law will act. If they're in a mood, I could end up in the hoosegow. It won't matter if I'm innocent or not.

I mount up and ride out of there.

Chapter 4

I ride on down the street in the rain. I've got a lot of questions. Who were those men? What's the map to? Who sent me the map and why?

I'm tempted to throw the damned thing away. I can already tell it's going to be nothing but trouble. The smart money would have been to give them the map. But I had to go and get all pig-headed and now I'm stuck. Even if I toss the map in the next puddle, I won't shake my troubles. They'll still think I have it.

Best thing I can do is lay low for a bit. Take cover and try to sort this all out.

I turn Coyote down the next street. It's near dark. The rain seems to be letting up a bit. Not that it matters. I'm wet all the way through now.

The streets are mostly empty. The few people I see are hurrying with their heads down. There's a wagon stuck in the mud, three men and a worn-out mule trying to get it out. The street goes downhill. The buildings around me get meaner and dirtier. A man stands in the shadows of a doorway, staring at me. I put one of my pistols in the pocket of my duster where I can get to it.

I come to a cheap lodging house. Two men are standing out front sharing a cigar. One of the windows opens on the upper floor and a woman dumps a bucket of wash water out onto the street.

I ride on by. Cheap as the place is, it's too rich for me. When that newspaper man offered to pay me for my story, I thought I'd hit the mother lode. I didn't realize that fifty dollars doesn't go far in this city. I found that out the hard way the first night when I celebrated by heading out for a steak dinner and a bottle of stump juice. I still can't believe it cost me ten dollars.

I keep heading downhill. The puddles are more like rivers down here. They're carrying all kinds of trash and things that have been dead a while.

The signs on the buildings change. There's no English on any of them now, only some peculiar symbols that I've come to learn are Chinese. For the life of me I can't make heads nor tails of any of them.

This is Chinatown. The only place in the city where I could find a room I could afford. It's a whole different world. The people I see are dressed different. Loose, flowing clothes. Conical hats with no brim. The first time I came down here I couldn't stop staring. I'd never seen people dressed like that.

They did a fair bit of staring at me too. It turns out not many people come down here who aren't Chinese. One night in the saloon I told a man where I was staying. He spat on the floor and told me they were dirty heathens and I should stay away from them.

He was wearing woolen long underwear that wasn't much besides dirt and holes, and there was something that looked like pieces of dead rat stuck in his beard. I didn't pay him any mind.

I pass through the market area. There's a lot of little stalls here, where the Chinese sell all kinds of things, most of which I've never seen before. They're all closed up now, except for one. It's got a tiny counter with three stools pulled up to it and a piece of tin for a roof. Behind the counter is an old woman standing at a stove made out of an old barrel. There's a pot of soup bubbling over the fire, steam rising off it.

I catch a whiff of the soup and my stomach starts fussing. I haven't had anything to eat all day and there's nothing to eat in my room.

The old woman's name is Li. She smiles at me and serves up a big bowl of soup. I set two bits on the counter and dig in. I don't know what all is in it, but it tastes good. While I eat, Li chatters away at me. It doesn't seem to matter to her that I don't know a word she's saying. I nod now and then and it's enough for her.

Down the street is a tiny house tucked in between two much larger buildings. I pull my saddlebags and my rifle and knock on the door. The old man who lives there comes out. His name is Qiang. He stables Coyote in his back yard, which isn't much bigger than a saddle blanket. It has a little overhang where Coyote can get out of the rain.

When I first started stabling Coyote here, I was worried. Coyote hates pretty much everybody. I was afraid he'd bite or stomp Qiang, and then I'd have all of Chinatown after me, screaming for blood.

But for some strange reason, Coyote likes Qiang. He follows the old man like a kitten around the side of the house. That horse never fails to surprise me.

The place I'm staying in is four stories of warped wood trying to figure out which direction to fall. The bottom floor is some kind of seamstress shop. The second floor is a laundry. I don't know what's on the third floor, except that they seem to use a lot of gunpowder. My room is on the fourth floor. A bunch of clotheslines are strung from my building to the tenement across the alley.

The stairs are on the outside. They sag and make alarming groaning noises every time I use them. So far I haven't fallen to my death, but every time I'm surprised to make it to the top in one piece.

The top floor is all one big room. Most of it is filled with stacks of crates and boxes and such. I'm not sure how they got all this stuff up here, especially with those stairs like they are.

The space I live in is in the far corner. I have to make my way down a narrow path between the boxes to get to it. A little bit of light comes in through the windows, which are covered with a thick layer of dirt and spider webs.

There's a small wood-burning stove in one corner. A table with a box pulled up to it that I use for a chair. Against one wall is a narrow cot with a straw-filled mattress. In the back corner is a ladder leading up to a trap door that lets onto the roof.

I change into some dry clothes and hang the wet ones up to dry. I light the kerosene lantern and lay my Colts on the table. As much as I want to look at the map, I need to clean and oil my guns first.

When I'm done with that, I take the map and spread it out on the table. It doesn't look much like any map I've ever seen. It's mostly words, some language I don't know. There are a couple of drawings, what looks like a mountain and something that looks like ruins. There's also a drawing of an owl. It's ragged along one edge, and when I look closer, I can see that it's torn there. So part of the map is missing.

What's it a map to? The postman said the letter came from Peru, so probably someplace there. It's got to be some kind of treasure map. Why else would people be willing to kill for it?

Damn it. I should burn the thing right now. If I've learned anything after that whole mess with the temple of the Aztec god Xipe Totec, it's that treasure is nothing but trouble.

But I know I won't do it. I might need it as a bargaining chip.

I turn it over. There's nothing on the back. I look in the envelope. Nothing there, either. Who sent it to me? And why? I don't know anyone in Peru. I don't even know where it is, except that it's a long way south.

I put the map back in the envelope and start to put it back in my saddlebags. Then I change my mind. That's probably not the best place for it. One thing about this room, there's lots of hiding places. I slide it between two of the crates.

I lie down on the cot and spend a few minutes staring up at the ceiling, trying to figure it all out. None of this makes any sense. Who would send me a map? And why?

Somewhere along the line I fall asleep. I wake up some time later and realize something.

There's someone in my room.

Chapter 5

The rain has stopped. Moonlight is coming in through the windows. I can see a dark figure over by the table. I reach for my gun belt, which I always hang on a nail by my bed.

My holsters are empty. The Colts are still lying on the table. Shoot.

I ease out of bed, moving slow so it doesn't creak. But it still makes some sound because the figure freezes and turns my way. There's no way he can see me tucked into this dark corner. He starts moving my way. I see the flash of moonlight on a gun barrel.

I soft foot it between two high stacks of crates. My bare feet make no sound. I'm glad I'm not wearing my boots.

The man comes closer. He's standing right by my bed now, looking down at it. I consider jumping him, then realize I've got a better idea.

I push one of the stacks over on him.

There's a huge crash and a yelp from him. He goes down, his gun skidding off into the darkness out of sight. A couple of the crates smash open. Their contents spill across the floor.

I hear voices and running footsteps. I should have known he wouldn't be alone. I'm about to run when I see that the stuff spilled on the floor looks familiar. It's hard to tell in the poor light, but it looks like it might be dynamite.

What's dynamite doing in here?

No time for that. I grab up a handful and duck back into the stacks as two men show up waving guns. I slip deeper into the shadows as they spread out, looking for me.

I head for the door. There's at least two armed men in here. I don't like the odds.

I make my way through the stacks until I can see the door. There's a man standing there, his back to the door, facing me. It's hard to tell, but it looks like he's holding a shotgun. Rushing him seems like a bad idea.

What about the dynamite? I haven't had such good luck with this stuff in the past, but I'm low on options. I reach into my pocket and feel a box of matches there. At least I didn't leave them on the table too.

I back away and find a spot where moonlight spills through a window. I look at the dynamite and realize I was wrong. It's not dynamite after all. It's fireworks, some kind of rockets. I saw the same kind one night last week here in Chinatown. They were having some kind of celebration, with a parade, big, paper dragons, music. And lots of fireworks.

I'm starting to get an idea.

I climb up on top of one of the stacks. Most of them are close enough together that I should be able to move around the room pretty easily. I jump to the next stack. It sways badly and almost tips over.

From there I can step to the next one and the next. In a few moments I'm back over to the door. I hunker down, scratch one of the matches to life, and light one of the rockets. The fuse burns fast, and I barely have time to point it at the man guarding the door before it takes off.

He looks up right before it hits him.

About a heartbeat later it explodes.

There's a loud bang and a huge explosion of colored lights. He screams and starts jumping around, swatting at his hair, which is on fire.

Before I can get down there, one of the other men comes running out of the stacks, a gun in his hand. I duck back out of sight.

Another man joins them. I keep some boxes between us so they can't see me and light another rocket. It shoots off toward them and explodes. A whole bunch of cursing follows, along with a few bullets, fired randomly in my direction.

But I'm already moving. There's another way out of here. I didn't want to use it, but it doesn't look like I have much choice unless I want to jump out a window. Four stories is a long way to fall.

I get to the open area where my bed and other stuff are. I can see the ladder up to the trapdoor. But there's a man here, turning this way and that, a shotgun ready in his hands. I think it's the one I dropped the stack on. Scattered around him on the floor are a whole mess of fireworks.

I duck back and light the last rocket. I pop up. He spins toward me and fires wildly. Buckshot spatters around me.

The rocket shoots toward him. His eyes get real big.

There's a huge bang and a flash of light. Then a bunch of the other fireworks start going off. The man howls and dances around crazily. They're blowing up all around him.

I'd like to stay and enjoy the show, but it's time to scoot while the scooting's good.

I run for the ladder. I knock the trapdoor out of the way and burst up onto the roof. I hear a shout and a bullet chips the wood near my face. These guys are getting way too close.

Instead of running, I wait by the trap door. A few seconds later a man's head pops up. I kick him, and he falls back down the ladder.

Then they start shooting into the ceiling. The thin wood doesn't do much to stop the bullets, which are popping up around my feet, so I decide it's time to run again.

The problem is, there's not really any place to run to.

There's a chimney sticking up over by one corner. I could hide behind it, but then what? They're going to have me trapped up here.

I run over to the edge and look down. About ten feet down is the outside stairway. I really don't want to jump down on it. It's almost sure to collapse under me.

A man appears through the trapdoor and starts shooting. That makes things a lot clearer. Rickety stairs beat hot lead any day.

I jump over the edge.

I land hard and go to my knees. The stairway shudders. Wood cracks. The whole thing sways drunkenly.

But it doesn't fall.

What do you know? It looks like something finally went my way.

Sure, I'm barefoot and unarmed and there are bad men chasing me with guns. But I'm not trapped anymore.

The door opens. The man who was guarding it from the inside is standing there. Even in the moonlight I can see that most of his hair is burned off. Some of it is still smoldering.

He steps out onto the landing.

And the whole stairway gives way…

Chapter 6

The stairway doesn't sort of fall. It basically disintegrates. One second I'm standing on it, the next I'm falling.

But I was expecting this, and I'm already moving.

I push off and get a hand on one of the clotheslines strung across the alley between this building and the tenements next door. It sags badly under my weight, but it's strong and it doesn't give way.

Until the man grabs onto my leg.

He only hangs on for a moment, but it's enough to snap the clothesline.

Now I'm swinging through the air, holding onto a broken clothesline, heading fast for the tenement building. The man falls away into darkness.

The impact is both better and worse than I thought. I thought I'd smack into the wall. I figured it would hurt a lot, but as long as I didn't let go of the line, I'd be okay.

Instead I smash through a window. Glass sprays everywhere, and I get a few new cuts on my face and arms.

I hit the floor in a darkened room and roll, coming up hard against the far wall. I stand up. I'm more than a little woozy. Glass cuts my bare feet.

A door opens and a shirtless man comes running into the room, yelling. I'm guessing this is his place. He doesn't look too happy to see me.

How do I know this? Because he's carrying a big meat cleaver and whatever he's shouting in Chinese, I'm pretty sure it isn't "Welcome, you want a cup of coffee?"

I snatch up the first thing I can lay my hands on, a chair. I get it up in time that the cleaver hits it instead of my head. The blade sticks in the wood. I shove the man backwards. While he's off balance, I sweep his feet out from under him.

Time to get out of here.

But now there's two women in the room too. One's old, probably his mother. The other looks like his wife.

The wife is swinging a broom. She lets me have a solid one on the side of the head. The mother throws a heavy mug right behind it. I manage to slap it away, but the plate that follows hits me in the chest hard enough to hurt.

Damn. These three are more dangerous than the men trying to kill me.

I snatch the broom away from the wife and use it to buy myself a bit of breathing room, enough to get out into the hallway. I slam the door behind me right as something heavy strikes it. That sounded like a frying pan.

I run down the hall. Every step hurts from the broken glass in my feet. This would have been a good night to fall asleep with my boots on.

I pause at the top of the stairs. I can hear someone running up the stairs toward me. Either they left another guard outside the building to stop me if I got past them, or the man who fell off the stairs is tough as hell.

I see the gun in his hands and decide it doesn't matter. I've got to get past him one way or another and fast, before more show up.

He's only one landing down, coming up fast. I consider jumping down on his head, but there's so many ways that could end up with me having a broken leg.

Then I see the cat. Its sitting by the railing, looking down at the man.

"Sorry about this," I say.

I pick up the cat—

And drop it on the man's head.

The cat yowls angrily. Claws flash. The man screams and starts flailing at the cat. He loses his footing and falls down the stairs. The cat jumps free.

I go running down the stairs. On my way by the cat, it lets me have it, scratching my leg deeply.

Okay, I deserve that.

The man isn't moving. I slip outside and hide in the darkness.

Chapter 7

I watch from the shadows until the men leave. By then it's getting near dawn. I'm cold and wet and I hurt all over.

And I still don't know why.

Who are those guys? Who sent them? Why do they want the map so bad?

Actually, I can guess the answer to that last question. It's a treasure map. Treasure makes men crazy. I've seen it over and over again.

It's not something I understand. Gold is nice and all. It buys food and bullets for my gun. But I don't want anything I can't carry on the back of a horse. I don't like things holding me down, and treasure to me seems like a big old stone trying to drag me to the bottom of the river.

It's not a lot of fun climbing up the side of the building back to my room. I pick through the wreckage and gather up my gear. Last I dig out the envelope with the map in it, tuck it inside my coat and head out into the morning.

I go to Qiang's, pay him and saddle up Coyote. It's long past time to leave this town. I'm heading south where it's warmer and people don't shoot at me. At least not as much.

I'm about to mount up when a voice behind me says, "Mister?"

I spin, my gun leaping into my hand.

The boy standing there turns white. "Don't shoot, mister!" he squawks. "Don't shoot!"

I holster my gun and smile at the boy to calm him. It doesn't really work. He still looks like a rabbit about to bolt into its hole.

"What do you want?" I ask him.

"You...you're Ace Lone Wolf, ain't you?" he stutters.

Now I'm suspicious again. I look around but don't see anyone hiding in the shadows waiting to shoot me. "How do you know that?"

"You're kind of famous," he says. His voice sounds better. He seems to be coming around to the idea that I'm not going to shoot him. "And you're the only Apache living in Chinatown."

He's got a point there.

"Why are you looking for me?"

"I got a telegram for you." For the first time I notice the folded piece of paper in his hand.

"A telegram?" He nods. I hold out my hand for it.

"It's four bits," he says, pulling the paper back. He sure got over being scared quick.

I put the money in his hand and take the telegram. First a letter, and now a telegram. I hesitate before unfolding it. I feel like I'm standing at a crossroads here. I could throw the telegram in the mud—along with the map—and ride away. If I ride fast enough and far enough, none of this will touch me.

But I know my curiosity won't let me do that. I have to know what's going on.

It says:

Bring the map to Lima, Peru. Stop.

Or they will kill me. Stop.

Then I see the name at the bottom.

Jack Palmer.

That's my father.

For a while all I can do is sit there and stare at it. What's he gotten himself into this time? I wonder.

I haven't seen my father in years, since the last time he stumbled into Pa-Gotzin-Kay—the ancient Apache stronghold in the Sierra Madre Mountains where I grew up. He had a stab wound in his shoulder, and he needed a place to hole up and heal. My mother spoke to the council and they agreed to let him stay in an empty wikiup.

I remember it clearly. I must have been about twelve at the time. I was so excited to see him. It had been years since I'd seen him, and I could barely remember him. There was so much I wanted to tell him, so much I wanted to show him.

It was good at first. He acted like he cared. He listened to what I had to say, followed me when I led him around. He talked a good game too. Started telling me all the things we were going to do together, all the things he was going to teach me to do.

He wasn't all talk. He showed me how to play cards. Showed me how to deal off the bottom of the deck, how to hide a card in your sleeve. I practiced hard. The first time I was able to do it correctly he smiled and ruffled my hair. That meant a lot to me.

Then one morning he just up and left. When I asked him why, he said, "I've got places to go, bucko."

"But you barely got here. You said you were—"

"Next time," he said. "I promise."

I ran after him as he rode away. I climbed up on the rocks and stared after him as he disappeared down the trail.

But he didn't come back.

First, I was sad. I moped around like a dogey calf looking for its mama. Then I got angry. I was angry for a long time.

I'm not angry anymore. I'm not anything anymore. As far as I'm concerned, I never had a father. Never needed one either. There was a guy I knew for a while, but he wasn't my pa. He was just another drifter blowing through like a tumbleweed.

I wad up the telegram. This is just like Jack, I think. He disappears until he wants something. Once he's got what he needs, he leaves. Whatever he's gotten himself into this time, I'm not getting involved. I throw the telegram on the ground and mount up.

It's time to get the hell out of Dodge.

I'm almost to the outskirts of the city when I start swearing and rein Coyote to a halt.

This is bull shit. He's using me. Jack Palmer is a bunco artist, through and through. If I get involved with him, I'm sure enough going to regret it.

I'm calling myself every name in the book as I turn Coyote around and head for the docks.

I've gotta be the dumbest man alive. But I can't turn my back on him.

There's really something wrong with me.

Chapter 8

The sea is calm, and the sun is shining when the ship docks in Lima. I'm the first person off. The ship has barely stopped moving before I jump onto the dock. It feels so good to have something solid underfoot. If I never get on a ship again, it will be too soon. I wonder how long it takes to ride from Peru back to Arizona.

We went through one hell of a storm a few days back. At first, I was afraid I was going to die. Then I got seasick something fierce, and I was afraid I wouldn't die. I never threw up so much in my life. I'm surprised there's anything left of me.

I have to wait for Coyote to be unloaded. He bites two of the crew on his way out. When I take hold of his bridle, he tries to bite me too.

"I know," I tell him. "I didn't much like it either." He snorts and narrows his eyes. He's telling me that however bad it was for me, at least I wasn't stuck down in the hold with a herd of sheep. He has a special hatred for sheep.

"What was I supposed to do?" I say. "He's a sonofabitch, but he's kin. I can't turn my back on him. It's not how I am." I've had this same argument with myself a hundred times since we left San Francisco. Coyote swishes his tail and stomps his foot. He's a long way from convinced.

So am I.

I saddle Coyote and mount up. Then I sit there, looking around. Seagulls wheel and screech overhead. Waves slap against the hulls of ships. Sailors and dockworkers hustle this way and that, shuffling cargo to and from the ships. Men shout. Donkeys bray and sheep bleat.

There's no sign of my father. Not that I expected to see him. I'm not sure what I expected, to tell the truth. It occurs to me that I might be too late. Maybe this time he finally got in over his head. Maybe he's dead.

There's no point in thinking that way. I need to do something.

23

I can see the city of Lima north of me. It sits on top of some low, steep-sided bluffs overlooking the ocean. It's not as big as San Francisco, but it's still bigger than every other place I've been. In the middle of the city is a section packed with tall buildings. I see a church bell tower. The part of the city closest to me looks to be all run-down shacks jammed tight together. I'd say that's the poor part of town.

I guess I'll head on into the city and start asking around. Jack's not the quiet type. He draws a lot of attention. Someone will have seen him. Fortunately, the people here speak Spanish, so at least I can talk to them.

There's a cluster of street vendors crowded around the street leading to the city, hawking food and drink to the sailors and passengers. I make my way through them, hoping Coyote doesn't kick anyone. When he's in a mood, there's no telling what he'll do.

I'm about the only person in the crowd on horseback, making it easy to see over the crowd. I go slow, not wanting to run anyone over. One nearby vendor draws my eye. She's a middle-aged woman, not very tall. Her hair is done up in an elaborate bun on top of her head and she's wearing a brightly-colored, hand-woven dress with long sleeves. She's cooking some little flat breads on top of an old drum.

What makes me look at her is the man standing at her stall. He's wearing a long, black, woolen coat that hangs almost to his ankles, and a wide-brimmed hat with silver braid on it. Something in the way he's standing tells me he's no ordinary customer.

I'm close enough to hear what he says.

"It's not enough," he says in Spanish. The accent is different than what I'm used to. It reminds me of the men who attacked me in San Francisco. He's holding some coins in his hand.

"It's all I have. Business is bad. The storm drove the ships away." She's afraid, but she's staring him in the eye and she's not backing down. This is a woman who doesn't push around easy.

"That's not my problem," he growls. "El Chacal, he isn't going to like this."

She crosses her arms. "I can't give him what I don't have."

24

"I don't like the way you talk to me." He puts his hands on her stall and gives it a little shake. "Be a shame if something was to happen to this."

"Break it and I'll have no way to pay your boss. What will he say then?"

He leans forward. He's got a badly pockmarked face and thick forearms gnarled with scars. "He'll say next I should break your arms." He cocks his head to the side. "Or maybe the arms of one of your grandchildren. How would you like that, eh?"

For the first time I see real fear in her eyes. "You leave the children alone!"

"Then you pay the money you owe." He reaches over, takes some of the food she's cooking, and shoves it in his mouth. "You have the money next week—*all* the money—or something bad happens to one of your grandbabies. That's a fact." Still chewing, he lumbers away to a nearby stall.

"I want to shoot him, Coyote," I say. Coyote twitches an ear toward me. He doesn't like bullies either. "I don't think anyone would mind, do you?" People move away from the man without looking at him. Probably he's shaking all of them down.

But on the corner up ahead is a soldier in a green uniform with a white belt. He has a rifle on a sling hanging over his shoulder, a bayonet attached to it. He's not doing anything to interfere with the pockmarked man, but that doesn't mean he'll stand by if I start shooting.

I move my hand away from my gun and keep moving.

I come to a saloon. It doesn't look much like the saloons where I come from, but that's sure enough what it is. Loud, drunken laughter comes from inside. A man stumbles out the door, trips over his feet, and sprawls on the ground. He lies there without moving.

I'm about to ride on by when a thought occurs to me. Where there's a saloon, there's gambling. And there's nothing that Jack likes better than gambling. He could be inside.

I ride up to the hitching rail and get down. There's only one other horse tied there, a roan mare at the far end.

I grab Coyote's nose. He's already giving the other horse the stinkeye. "Leave him alone, Coyote. I mean it."

He snorts and rolls his eyes at me. But he doesn't go straight after the other horse. I hope it's enough. It's the best I'm going to get.

The saloon is a sprawling building with walls made of scraps of driftwood and tin. The roof is nothing more than a large canvas held up in the middle by a support post. I'm not sure what's holding the place up. It looks like it could blow away into the sea any minute.

Sitting outside, leaning up against the wall, is a man dressed in stained white clothing. His face is lined by the years, his eyes bloodshot.

He raises a hand as I reach for the door. "It's a bad place," he says in Spanish. "You don't want to go in there."

"Probably not," I say. "But I reckon I have to."

The door is a sheet of canvas tacked onto a flimsy wooden frame. There's something red splashed on it that's probably blood. I take a deep breath and go on in.

Chapter 9

It's dim inside, the only light coming in through gaps in the walls. I guess windows were too much trouble. I stand there for a minute, letting my eyes adjust. I'm in a big, open room, and it's crowded. There's a bar made of planks laid over wooden barrels running the whole length of the back wall. The bartender is a big, bald man with thick arms.

It smells. Bad. The place is full of sailors and dockworkers. I hear at least five different languages and see all manner of strange dress. The floor is dirt, though someone threw straw down to try and soak up some of the spilled alcohol, blood and vomit. It's not working all that well.

Looks like Jack's kind of place.

I make my way through the crowd, stepping over a man lying on the floor, unconscious or dead. I don't stop to check. Someone falls into me from behind, causing me to bang into a big, square-headed man with an eyepatch. He bares his teeth at me and draws a wicked, curved knife from his belt.

But I've been expecting something like this. My left hand comes up holding a Colt, which I shove up to his nose. He smiles and nods, then steps aside like he's motioning me through a door. The knife goes back into his belt.

I pass by a table with a number of men crowded around it. Sitting at the table is a man with a long, braided beard. He has his left hand spread out on the table top. With his right hand, he's stabbing a knife between his fingers, moving back and forth. He's going so fast the knife is a blur. Somehow, he manages not to stab himself in the hand. It's impressive. Stupid, but impressive.

The others around the table are throwing down bets and arguing amongst themselves.

Then a squat, barefoot man wearing a bandanna wrapped around his head, his face weathered by a lifetime at sea, deliberately bangs into his arm. The bearded man stabs himself in the back of the hand and bellows.

He leaps to his feet, yanks the knife out of his hand, and throws himself at the squat man. The two go down on the floor, cursing and stabbing at each other. Others laugh and kick them.

What a great place.

Then I see him. It's been almost ten years, but I'd recognize him anywhere. He's got straight blond hair that falls to his shoulders and a neatly-trimmed goatee. He's wearing a tight-fitting black coat over a white shirt and a black string tie. In a room filled with rough-looking characters, he looks out of place.

He's sitting at a table near the middle of the room with four other men. Cards and cash and alcohol cover the table. He's staring at his hand, stroking his goatee.

I feel my anger start to rise. I should have known I'd find him gambling. So much for being in mortal danger.

I give up being polite and shove my way through the crowd. Someone swears when I step on his foot and pushes me. I shove my pistol in his face with a snarl. He puts up his hands and backs away.

Jack and a dark-skinned man dressed in rough dungarees, a gold ring in his nose, are the only ones still playing when I get to the table. Jack lays his cards down, showing three of a kind to the man's two pair. Jack reaches for the pile of money in the middle of the table. The man with the nose ring suddenly swears and jumps up. He has a machete hanging from his belt. He rips it free and starts waving it at Jack and yelling.

Jack sits there calmly, his hat pushed back, a little smile on his face. That only makes the man madder.

"I'll kill you, you dirty cheater!" the man screams.

"You're getting all heated up over nothing," Jack replies. He has just a hint of a drawl. "It's a friendly game."

I stop, waiting to see how it all unfolds. The room has gone quiet. Men are pushing closer, blood in their eyes. I see a lot of unfriendly looks turned on Jack. He's made more than one enemy in this room.

"Maybe I cut your cheating hands off. You still think it's friendly then?" Nose Ring steps closer, raising the machete.

"Now, now," Jack says, still calm. He's leaning back a bit in his chair. He looks like he's sitting on the porch with an old friend, not facing a maddened enemy. "You're not thinking clearly. Maybe this will help." He brings his hand up from under the table. He's holding a pistol. "There's no cheating here. You're angry is all. Once you calm down, you'll see sense again."

Nose Ring is breathing hard. His knuckles are white, he's gripping the machete so tightly. But he comes no closer. His eyes are fixed on Jack's gun.

"How about you sit back down, and we forget this ever happened? No one needs to get shot here. Who knows? You might actually win your money back."

For a moment I think Nose Ring is going to attack him anyway. He's so angry his eyes are actually red. Then he gets this black smile on his face.

"How about this instead? We kill you and I take back all the money you cheated me out of." As he says this, he jerks his chin. When he does, about ten of the men who are crowded around all draw their guns and point them at my father.

Oops. This just got sticky.

None of them are looking at me. I could shoot three or four quick as a wink. But the last thing I want to do is start blazing away. Ten-to-two is bad odds no matter how you cut the deck. And there's no way of knowing how many other men in here will pull guns and start throwing lead around. A body could pick up a passel of new holes in the confusion.

This is going to get downright ugly.

Someone needs to tell Jack that. He's still not backing down. His gun is steady, and he has a big smile on his face like this is just another fun afternoon in the sun. Who knows? Maybe for him it is. I don't know why nobody's killed him yet.

I look around, trying to come up with something I can do. That's when I realize I'm standing next to a post. I scan the room. I do believe it's the only thing holding up the canvas roof.

"Are you sure that's how you want this to go?" Jack asks, shaking his head a little like he can't believe this foolishness. With his free hand, he counts the men facing him. "That's only eleven. Are you sure you don't need more help?"

Nose Ring jerks his chin again. Three more men step forward. The sound of them cocking their pistols is loud in the still air.

Dammit, Jack. Just shut up already.

29

Jack sighs. He sounds like a man who's trying his best to be patient. He's about two shakes of a lamb's tail from getting shot to doll rags. Time to act.

I sure hope this works.

I turn and kick in the same motion, putting everything I have into it. There's a loud crack as the post gives way—

For a moment nothing happens. Half the guns swing to me, and I have a sudden feeling I made a big mistake.

Then the roof comes down.

Chapter 10

The canvas settles down on the room. Everything goes dark. Shouts go up, and a couple of shots ring out. The canvas is surprisingly heavy. It's hard to stand up under it. I crouch and move toward where I saw Jack last. I have both my guns out.

I find him still at the table. He's trying to hold the canvas up with one hand, while with the other he's scooping up money.

"What are you doing? Let's get out of here!" I yell at him.

"I'm getting my money," he yells back. He doesn't seem surprised to see me.

I grab his arm and pull on him. "There's no time."

"There's always time for money."

The canvas lifts up a bit, and there's Nose Ring again. He howls and swings at Jack. I'm half tempted to do nothing. I'm sure Jack deserves it.

Instead, I shoot him in the leg.

He goes down. More shots go off as his friends surge toward us. A bullet whizzes by my ear.

"Stay then," I tell Jack. I can't believe I risked my life to help him. "But I'm getting out of here."

Jack scoops one last handful of money and comes after me. All around us are cursing, struggling men. It's hard to move very fast, hunched over like this. I'm not sure I'm even heading for the door.

Someone bangs into me from the side, almost knocking me down. He tries to punch me, but he can't get much behind it. I smack him in the face with the butt of my gun, and he decides he'd be better off going after someone else.

We get to a spot that's a little less crowded. I see a man still sitting at his table. He's the only one. Everyone else is trying to get out of there. He's quickly downing the drinks they left behind.

There's a man who's got his priorities in order. Whether they're good priorities is another matter.

"I kill you!" someone screams from behind us. It sounds like Nose Ring. I hope I never see him again.

Daylight ahead and a moment later we stumble out into the sunlight. Dozens of other men have already made it out and more are emerging every second. The saloon is a sea of canvas, rippling from underneath.

"Luis is going to be so mad at you," Jack says.

I turn to him, confused. "Who's Luis?"

"The man who owns that bar. You just cost him a lot of money."

"Me? I was trying to save you."

"That won't matter much to him."

There's a puff of smoke as the canvas starts to burn in one, then two, places. That'd be from the kerosene lamps. They're good for light, but bad for fires.

"Probably time to go," Jack says.

"You think?"

Right then Nose Ring pops out the door. He's leaning on one of his compadres. He curses and raises his machete. I kick him. He tumbles backward into the doorway, knocking down two other men as he goes.

I'm making more friends by the second. I ought to run for mayor.

I run to Coyote. Jack jumps on the roan mare.

"Follow me!" he yells.

He gallops up the dirt street, heading uphill toward the city. I follow, ducking low in case anyone starts shooting.

We make it up the bluffs and into the city. No one seems to be following us. We slow to a walk. Jack looks Coyote up and down and frowns.

"You sure picked an ugly one to steal."

"I didn't steal Coyote!" I snap, not liking how my voice rises. "I brought him from San Francisco. And he's not ugly," I add, even though he really kind of is. He's a dirty yellow color. He's got a jug head, crazy eyes and stubby legs. But he doesn't look ugly to me. "He's got more heart than ten other horses put together."

"Huh," Jack says. He's not convinced. "So you brought him all the way from San Francisco. Why'd you do that? They have horses here, you know."

"Coyote isn't just any horse." I pause, trying to figure out how to put it into words. How can I tell him about the bond Coyote and I have? The things we've been through together. All the times he's saved my bacon. He'll never understand. "He's different, is all. Where I go, he goes. Unless he decides to leave. I won't stop him if he does."

He looks at me, raising an eyebrow. "Is this some kind of Apache thing? I never heard anyone else in the clan talk like that about their horse."

"No. It's not. It's my thing. I don't want to talk about it with you."

Jack shrugs. "I don't remember you being so touchy."

"I'm surprised you remember me at all, it's been so long."

"Fair enough," he says placidly. "You got the map?"

"Yeah, I got the map."

"Where is it?"

It's in my saddlebags, but I make no move to get it out. Instead, I say, "Your telegram said they were going to kill you if I didn't rush down here with the map. But when I get here, I find you gambling!" Darn it. It happened again. My voice keeps jumping up like one of those silly little dogs I saw the rich women carrying around in San Francisco.

He nods. "I needed to make sure you'd come," he says.

"You were gambling!"

"I was waiting for your ship. But then I got bored. It was only a bit of harmless fun."

"Harmless? You nearly got both of us killed."

He makes this gesture like he's waving off a fly, like facing an angry mob in a saloon is no big deal. "You're exaggerating. It was a little misunderstanding is all."

"I don't think the man with the nose ring saw it that way."

"Batiste? He's got a problem with his temper. He'll get over it."

"How are you not dead yet?"

He flashes me that famous smile, all white teeth and a twinkle in his eye. "It's my charming personality that saves me. That and a bit of luck, the luck of the Irish."

"You're not Irish."

"So I can't have any of their luck?"

33

"Why didn't you just tell me to mail the map back to you?" I ask.

"I don't know. That sounds like a good way to lose it. You know how unreliable the mail is."

"If it's so unreliable, then why'd you mail it to me?" Shoot. There goes my voice, getting away from me again. I can't believe how badly I want to wring Jack's neck. I've only been around him for what, five minutes?

He spreads his hands. "I was in a tight spot. Some bad *hombres* were closing in. I had to think fast. I couldn't let it fall into their hands."

"And you thought it would be a good idea to mail it to me? You thought, hey, Ace is probably doing nothing. Why don't I get him mixed up with some people who will try and kill him too?"

"When you say it like that, it sounds bad."

"It *is* bad!"

"You're so dramatic. You've been in plenty of scrapes, I'm sure."

He's got me there. I haven't been living what you'd call a quiet life. Between hunting for lost Aztec temples, running from giant grizzly bears, getting chased by the US Cavalry and almost killed by ghosts on an old Spanish ship, I've had plenty of excitement since I left the stronghold.

He stops his horse. I do too. He puts his hand on my shoulder and looks me in the eye. "Ace, there was no one else I could trust."

That sticks in my chest somewhere. But I'm angry. I push his hand away. "That's crap. Don't pull that on me. I know how you are. Mother told me. You say and do whatever you think will get you what you want."

"That's true," he allows. "But what I said is also true." He takes a deep breath. "I'm in over my head on this one, son. I think I've known for a while that I needed your help on it."

He sounds so sincere that I almost fall for it. Instead, I shake my head. "Don't. Just don't."

"Don't what?"

"Do that thing you do."

"You see a lot of ghosts, Ace." He raises an eyebrow. "The map?"

34

I still don't reach for it. "How did you know where to find me, anyway?"

He grins. "This." He reaches into his coat, takes out a newspaper and hands it to me. It's not in good shape. It's been folded too many times and there's something red on it that's probably blood. It's folded so that my picture is right there on top. Under that is the story that newspaper man wrote about me.

"How'd you get this?" I ask.

He takes it back. "Lima isn't the end of the world. We get news here."

"I knew that story was a bad idea. I never even got paid all the money he promised me. He left town before he paid me the other twenty-five dollars."

"You're too trusting, son. That's always been one of your weaknesses."

"That's not true," I shoot back, trying not to think about how easily Victoria suckered me. "And stop talking like you know me. You don't know anything about me."

"I know you better than you think."

"How's that? You were never around."

"No, I wasn't." He sounds sad, but I'm not buying. "But even as a kid I could see the man you would grow up to be." He waves the paper at me. "I'm proud of you. I want you to know that."

I know he's just saying what he thinks will get me on board with him, but I can't deny it feels good anyway. I shake it off angrily.

"Try to look at this as another adventure. If half of what is in this story is true, you know how to handle yourself in a scrape. Together, we can do this."

"There's no together. I'm not helping you."

"But you haven't heard me out yet."

"It doesn't matter. Whatever snake oil you're selling, I'm not buying."

"You're upset."

"Darn tooting I'm upset!"

"That was cute," he says with another big grin.

"What was?"

"You said 'darn tooting'. That's cute."

"I hope Batiste catches up to us. This time I'm letting him have you."

"Can I have the map now, Ace?"

"Maybe I threw it in the ocean."

"We both know you didn't do that." He holds his hand out. "Please?"

Still grumbling, I reach into my saddlebag and pull it out.

He takes the map. "You left this in your saddlebags while you went into the saloon?" For the first time he seems flustered. "Are you crazy? People down there will steal anything that isn't nailed down, and even then…"

Now it's my turn to smile. "You don't know Coyote. The first man who tries to put his hand anywhere near him is going to lose some fingers. Then Coyote's going to make hoofprints on his chest."

Jack looks at Coyote differently, like he's seeing him for the first time. Coyote bares his teeth like he knows what we're saying. Who knows? Maybe he does.

"I think he just bared his teeth at me," Jack says.

"He did."

"Horses aren't supposed to do that."

"You try telling him that. Coyote does what he wants to."

"Remind me to keep my hands away from his mouth." He looks around to make sure no one is watching, takes the map out, glances at it, then puts it back.

"What's it the map to?" I ask.

He tucks the envelope inside his shirt. "You'll never believe—"

A shot rings out. Jack's hat flies off.

Chapter 11

I draw my guns and turn. There's two men riding toward us. One is short, pudgy, and very pale skinned. He's wearing glasses and a huge, floppy hat. The other one is tall and skinny with a scraggly beard. He's wearing a battered stovepipe hat.

They each fire as they come, but it's clear neither of them has done this much because the shots go wild. Really wild. The short one shoots into the ground near his horse's feet. The tall one nearly shoots the short one.

Turns out shooting from the back of a running horse is hard. Who knew?

The short one's horse doesn't like having a bullet bouncing around near his feet and he bucks a little. His rider grabs onto the saddle horn and drops his gun.

I could shoot them, but I don't. The way I see it, whatever beef they have with Jack is probably justified. I fire a couple of times over their heads to slow them up a bit and turn to Jack. The best thing to do is get out of here.

But Jack's not on his horse. He's down on the ground.

"What are you doing? Let's get out of here!" I yell.

"I'm not going without my hat." He clamps it on his head and jumps back in the saddle.

Another gunshot from our attackers. This one is close enough that I can hear it whine on the way by.

We take off running. I have a feeling this is something I'm going to do a lot around Jack.

We turn a corner and get out of the line of fire for a moment.

"Is there anyone in this city that doesn't want to kill you?" I yell at my father.

"You don't," he yells back.

"Are you sure about that?"

Coyote has his ears back. He's still mad about the boat ride and now he's got people shooting at him. He's going to make me pay for this, I'm sure of it. I better watch my fingers and toes.

We make it around another corner, run a couple more blocks, then take another corner. Jack points at a narrow lane between two tall buildings. "We can cut through there."

He rides in without waiting for an answer. The lane is choked with tall weeds and vines. We don't get very far before it dead ends at a brick wall.

"Oops," Jack says. We turn around and start to head out. We don't get far before we hear them coming. There's nothing to do now but hunker down and hope they don't see us.

We can hear them arguing.

"You shot too soon and scared him off, Myron," the tall one says. "I told you to wait until we got closer."

"I'm telling you, Lonnie, it was an accident. My finger slipped."

"You're an accident. I swear, if you weren't my brother, I'd shoot you myself. You're useless. Mama should have stopped after she had me."

"So now it's all my fault? I didn't see you hitting them either."

"You know I got a bad eye. If we got closer, I coulda used my shotgun."

"You couldn't hit the broad side of a barn with two shotguns."

"I'll show you how good I can shoot. Go on, try me."

They come to a stop near the mouth of the lane. If they look down here, they're sure to see us. The weeds give us some cover, but not much.

Lonnie, the tall one, says, "Now we gone and lost them." He takes off his battered stovepipe hat and wipes sweat from his forehead.

"They gotta be here somewhere," Myron says, peering around. His glasses are round and thick. The way he's squinting, I'm not sure he could see us even if he was looking straight at us.

"I'm telling you, we took a wrong turn. I told you we shoulda gone right back there."

A group of women come walking by then. They're dressed up fancy, with petticoats and little umbrellas to keep the sun off. Both men hastily put their guns away and doff their hats.

"Good afternoon, ladies," Lonnie says.

"A lovely day, ain't it?" Myron adds.

The women turn their faces away and hurry on by.

"You scare everyone off, don't you?" Myron says when they're gone. "It's that idiot hat you wear. I keep telling you to throw it away."

"It ain't my hat that's the problem," Lonnie snaps back. "It's that floppy thing you wear. It looks like something my grandma would wear in her garden. It ain't no kind of man's hat at all."

"You know I wear this hat on account of my fair skin," Myron protests. He has red hair and lots of freckles. "I burn easy. I can't help that."

"Why don't you wear a bonnet then? Better yet, just put a sack over your head."

"You're gonna go too far one of these days, Lonnie," Myron grumbles, pulling his hat down tighter and turning his horse to head back the way they'd come. "I keep warning you. Best you listen."

"Blah, blah, blah. All you do is talk. Why if I had a plugged nickel for every time you said..." He follows the shorter man out of sight. We can hear them still arguing.

"That was interesting," Jack says.

I look at him. "Interesting? That's what you have to say? Someone tried—"

I don't finish my sentence because right then a whole lot of water hits me out of nowhere, drenching me.

I look up to see a woman leaning out of an upstairs window. She's holding a wash bucket in her hands. She yells in Spanish, "Get out of my garden, idiots!"

I look down. Sure enough, we're standing in a little garden I never noticed before.

"My apologies, ma'am," Jack calls up to her. "We're leaving now."

We get out of there and back on the street. I notice Jack is laughing at me.

"It isn't funny."

"Looks pretty funny from where I'm sitting."

I empty water out of one of my boots. "She should have dumped the bucket on you. It was your dumb idea to go in there."

"I'm just lucky, I guess." I grumble some more. He says, "Come now. We'll go to a little place I know. I'll get you something to eat. That will cheer you right up."

Chapter 12

He leads me to this little mud brick place with a thatch roof. There's no door and no glass in the windows. We leave the horses out front and go inside.

The room's only big enough for about four people. There's a tiny table with an old man sitting at it, sipping something steaming out of a mug. A man in a badly stained apron is sweating over a stove with a couple of frying pans on it. He looks at Jack and gestures at the back door with the knife in his hand.

We go through the back door. There's a seating area out back, a handful of rickety tables and some rough-sawn stumps as chairs. There's men sitting at two of the tables. They look us over. One of them nods at Jack. They go back to their conversations.

"No one will bother us here," Jack says, heading for a table near the back. He drops onto the stump with a sigh.

He takes off his hat and puts a finger in the hole. "It's a damn shame. I was right fond of this hat."

"Who cares about your hat?" I say, pulling up the other stump. I'm feeling downright peevish. My boots squish when I walk and it's going to take all day for my pants to dry. "Two men just tried to shoot us and all you can think about is your hat?"

He makes that gesture again like he's waving off a fly. Like what I'm angry about is too small to even notice.

"You saw what poor shots they are," he says. "We were never in any real danger."

"Even a bad shot can get lucky," I say. "Who are they?"

"Common ruffians, I'd say," Jack says. "This city is infested with criminals. They must have gotten wind of the map somehow and figured they'd try to take it from us."

I shake my head. "No."

He raises an eyebrow. "No, what?"

"You said 'us'. There's no us. There's *you*. The map is your problem, not mine."

"Okay, okay." He puts his hands up. "No one's forcing you to do anything."

"No, you're only tricking me is all."

"You're still mad about that?" He says it like it's really something he can't grasp, that I would be mad about sailing halfway around the world based on a lie.

"Of course, I'm still mad! Why wouldn't I be?"

"I didn't know you were the type to hold a grudge is all. You must have gotten that from your mother."

"Don't you dare. You don't get to blame things on her."

"Relax. Have a beer. They make quite good beer here." About then the man in the apron sets two mugs down in front of us. Jack fishes out a coin and hands it to him. "Keep the change," he tells him. He looks at me. "I'm sorry about the deception. I made what seemed like the best choice at the time. But from here on out, it's complete honesty. Anything you want to know, all you have to do is ask and I'll tell you."

I don't believe him. Not a bit. What makes me angry, though, is I *want* to believe him. I hate that. "What's the map to?"

His eyes dart around, checking to see how far away everyone else is. He leans forward and lowers his voice. "It leads to a lost treasure." He says it very dramatically, then sits back, his expression saying he's waiting for me to be all impressed.

Instead, I cross my arms. "So?"

That surprises him. He frowns. "You don't think it's real?"

"Maybe it is, maybe it isn't. Either way, I'm not interested."

"What? How can you not be interested? It's the map to the lost treasure of Atahualpa, the last emperor of the Inca empire."

"Mountains of gold, right? Heaps of treasure?"

"No. It's a giant ruby called the Heart of the Empire."

"Still not interested."

"I'm starting to think there's something wrong with you," he says.

"I've chased treasure before. A couple of times. I'm not doing it again." I take a drink of my beer. It is pretty good.

"Why not?"

"Treasure is nothing but trouble. All you have is a map and look how much trouble you're having."

"But think what you could do with your share."

"Money doesn't spend when you're dead."

41

He does that thing again with his hand, like he's waving off a pesky fly. "You worry too much. With my brains and your skills, it's as good as done. Nothing can stop us."

"Stop saying us. There is no us."

"Look. I'm giving you the opportunity of a lifetime, here."

"No, you're not. You're trying to fast talk me into helping you."

"You don't trust me," he asks. His face says he's hurt by this, but I don't believe it.

"I just traveled halfway around the world because you lied to me! Would you believe you after that?"

"When you put it like that, it sounds bad."

"How else should I put it?"

"You could see it as your old pa offering you a chance of a lifetime. Think what you could do with your third of the treasure."

"Third? Not half?"

"Well, I did the hard part already, getting the map and all."

"You're something else, you know that?"

He grins. "I hear that a lot. I take it as a compliment."

"No way I'd do this for a third. That's insulting."

"But you *will* do it?"

"What makes you think that?"

"We're negotiating, aren't we? I can go thirty-five percent. That's my family deal. You should take it."

"Who did you steal it from?"

"What makes you think I stole it?"

"Because I know you."

"Where does this come from, Ace? Why are you so eager to believe the worst about me?"

"Let me see." I start ticking off the points on my fingers. "You abandoned my mother and me. Then you came back when you needed something. As soon as you got it, you left again. Oh, and you're a card cheat. Did I miss anything?"

"It's a lot more complicated than that."

I finish my beer. "Explain it to me then."

"I had to leave, don't you see?" He has kind of a desperate look on his face now. "I didn't fit in out there."

"You didn't fit in. That's a terrible excuse."

"You of all people should know it's not. You should know what I'm talking about. After all, you left too. You abandoned them too."

"I did not abandon them."

"No. From the story I read, it sure sounded like it. What do you call it then?"

"It wasn't abandoning them. I needed to…I don't know. I felt like…"

"Like you didn't fit. Ace, people like you and me, we're not like everyone else. We're wanderers. It's who we are. You can't cage a wolf and expect it to thrive." He winks. "I like the last name you came up with. Lone Wolf."

"That was just something I made up. It doesn't mean anything."

"Are you sure? Because I think it does. I think it means everything. You're a lone wolf just like your old man. Don't be mad about it. It's who you are."

"Talking with you is pointless. I brought you your map, Jack. Now I'm done. I'm leaving on the first ship I can hitch onto."

His face falls. "Did you say what I think you said? Did you call me Jack?"

"I did."

"But, I'm your dad. You should call me Pa. Father would be okay too."

I snort. "No chance. A father is someone who raises you, teaches you things."

He looks confused. "Like what kind of things?"

"I don't know. How to hunt or something. All you taught me was how to play cards."

"That's a kind of hunting."

"I'm talking about hunting for food."

"You can win money, buy food with that." He acts all proud, like he scored a point there.

"I don't want to talk about it anymore, Jack." I put emphasis on his name. He winces a little.

We're so busy arguing that we don't notice the men at the other tables have all gone quiet. The first sign I have of trouble is when a shadow falls over me. Irritated at being interrupted, I look up.

And up. And up.

There are two very large men standing over us. They look too much alike to be anything but brothers. They're bald and built like bulls. No necks. Small eyes sunk deep. Hands like hams. The matching black suits they're wearing probably took a whole field of cotton to make and it still looks like they're barely hanging on.

"You're coming with us," one of them says.

Chapter 13

I drop my hands to my guns. Jack puts up his hand to stop me.

"It's okay," he says.

I move my hands away. I'm not sure I have enough bullets to stop these men anyway. This close, they'd be sure to get their hands on me before they dropped. They'd tear me into little pieces.

Jack smiles up at them like they're old friends. "Chato. Gordo. It's good to see you boys again. We haven't finished our beers yet. Why don't you join us? I'm buying."

In answer, one leans over and picks up Jack's mug. It looks small in his hand. His expression stays completely flat as he squeezes the mug. It shatters. The big man opens his hand and lets the pieces fall on Jack.

"I wasn't thirsty anyway," Jack says. He stands up, brushing beer and pieces of pottery off himself. "Just me, or can my partner come too?"

"I'm not your partner."

A thick hand settles on my shoulder, and I'm lifted to my feet like a puppy.

"I guess I will come along," I say. "I don't have anything else to do right now."

The hand lets go. My shoulder feels like it was caught in a vise. My whole arm is tingling.

"You need to be careful with those things, Chato," I tell him. "Or is it Gordo?"

He stares at me flatly, his expression never changing.

"I'm glad we could have this talk," I say.

The men follow us through the place and back out into the street.

"We'll meet you there, Gordo," Jack says to the one who crushed his beer mug. "I take it El Chacal is still at the same place?"

Gordo shakes his head. He points. Across the street a coach is waiting. It's bigger than any coach I've ever seen. Looks like it could seat ten. It's painted red and gold. There are silk curtains at the windows. A team of six matched black horses is hitched to it. The driver is wearing a red uniform with lots of gold braid at the shoulders and white gloves. He stares straight ahead.

"I don't know," Jack says. "I'm a little sticky from the beer. I'm afraid I'd stain the seats. How about we meet you there?"

Instead of answering, Gordo pushes him toward the coach.

"You never were one for small talk, Gordo," Jack says. "You're the kind of man who gets right to the point. That's what I like about you."

Gordo pushes him again. Chato turns his big head to me. I put up my hands. "I'm coming. There's no need to get pushy."

The coach is even fancier on the inside. Every surface is covered in red satin. The seats are so deep in cushions I about sink out of sight when I sit down. Along the side is a bar with bottles of every kind of liquor ever made, with a little railing along the edge to keep them from rattling off.

Jack and I sit at one end. The brothers climb in. The whole coach sinks about a foot. They sit down at the other end, put their hands on their knees and stare at us.

"I've been wanting to ride in this," Jack says, rubbing his hands together. He actually looks happy. He looks the bar over and whistles in approval. "What can I pour you?" he asks.

"Nothing. I want to keep my wits about me."

"You're too serious. You need to lighten up and enjoy yourself. Life is short."

"Especially around you."

He pauses in the middle of pouring. "What? You're blaming me for this too?"

"Who else should I blame?"

"How was I supposed to know they would turn up?"

"What did you do?"

"Why do you always think the worst of me? What makes you think I did anything?"

I gesture at the two brothers. "They aren't here to invite you to a party."

He winces a little. "Okay. I can see how you'd take this the wrong way. But I'm telling you that you don't need to worry. They're friendly guys once you get to know them."

I look at the brothers. Neither has moved a muscle. I don't think they've so much as blinked.

"What's this about?" I ask.

He makes that motion again, like he's waving off a fly. I'm starting to hate when he does that. "It's a misunderstanding, that's all. El Chacal and I have a...business arrangement. A few loose ends to work out."

"What does *el chacal* mean?"

"It means The Jackal."

"What is that?"

"It's like a kind of wild dog, but really vicious. They run off lions sometimes."

"Sounds like a friendly sort," I say.

Jack sits back in his seat and takes a sip of his drink. "He's not too bad as long as you stay on his good side."

I'm thinking anyone who calls himself the Jackal doesn't have any good sides. "What does he do?"

"He's what you call a local businessman."

"That doesn't tell me anything. What's his business?"

"He has a finger in most every pie in town. But his core business is gambling. If there's gambling, he's getting a piece of it." He leans over and whispers, "It would be best if you didn't let slip how you wrecked Luis' saloon. You cost El Chacal a few sols with that little stunt." Sols are what they call their money here.

"*My* little stunt? You're the one who was cheating."

Jack holds up one finger. "Allegedly."

I sigh. He's impossible. "You owe the Jackal money, don't you?"

"A little."

One of the brothers cracks his knuckles. I don't know which one. I already forgot which was which. I get the feeling he's warming up to crack something else. "You owe more than a little, I bet."

"Depends on what you think is a little. It's all a matter of perspective. You'll learn that when you get older."

"*If.* If I get older. Being around you I'm not so sure."

47

"Don't worry so much. I'll take care of you. Just stick close."

"Nope. I'm getting away from you as soon as I can."

"I know you don't mean that." While we're talking, he's pouring himself another drink. He sinks back into the cushions, sips his drink, and sighs. "That's the good stuff."

"You seem pretty calm for someone who's about to get his arms twisted off."

"You have to enjoy the little things, son."

"Don't do that."

"Do what?"

"Act like you're sharing some great wisdom with me. You're not. You're a gambler and a hustler. There's nothing I want to learn from you."

His smile disappears. "You know how to cut a man deep."

I look at the brothers. "If you're going to knock him around, let me help, okay?" Still no response except the other one cracks his knuckles.

The coach stops after a bit. There's the sound of a gate opening. The coach rolls on through. We climb out and look around.

We're in a large courtyard, high, whitewashed walls all around. There are men wearing black coats standing around, all of them armed with pistols and shotguns. Tall, iron gates swing closed.

The brothers stick out their hands. "Your guns," one of them says. I can't tell which one. Neither one's mouth moved.

Jack and I unbuckle our gun belts and hand them over.

Chato—I think it's Chato anyway; he's slightly smaller than Gordo—points to an arched passageway. We go that way, the two brothers following. I swear I can feel the ground shaking as they walk.

Jack is admiring it all as we go. "See that?" he says, pointing at the statue of a man set in an alcove in the wall. It's made of some kind of white stone. He's not wearing anything except for what looks like a headband made of leaves. "That was imported from Italy. Ancient Roman. Very expensive."

"He's not wearing any clothes."

"That's how they made statues back then."

"I can't say I'd want to have a naked man standing around staring at me."

"That's because you have no culture, Ace. Don't take it hard, though. I know where you grew up."

"People feel like punching you a lot, I guess."

He shrugs. "More often than you'd think."

He's wrong about that.

The passageway leads us to another, smaller courtyard. Thick, lush plants heavy with flowers line the edges. In the middle of the courtyard is a small pool with a low, stone wall around it. Sitting at a table near the pool is a muscular man with long, bushy black hair. He's wearing an all-white suit. Everything is white, even his shoes. His shirt is unbuttoned halfway, showing a matt of thick chest hair. I'd bet anything he's El Chacal.

Standing in front of El Chacal is another man. He has his head down and he's holding his hat in his hands.

El Chacal looks at us and smiles, showing a whole lot of long, white teeth. "Jack, I'm glad you're here. I want you to see this."

El Chacal turns back to the man standing in front of him. His smile disappears. "Where were we? Yes, the money. Where is it? Where is my money, Esteban?"

Esteban twists his hat. "I didn't take it. I swear."

On the table in front of El Chacal is a plate with a steak on it. He stabs the steak and saws off a piece. "No? Who did?"

"I don't know. It wasn't me."

I notice that Chato and Gordo have moved up behind Esteban. Esteban notices too. He glances over his shoulder at them and goes pale.

El Chacal puts a piece of steak in his mouth and chews noisily. He looks over at us. "This is a really good steak," he says, his mouth still full of steak. "It has to be bloody, you know? Really bloody." Blood stains his teeth now. Some runs down his chin. He turns back to Esteban and points his knife at him.

"I want my damn money."

Esteban is shaking now. "I don't have it. I swear!"

El Chacal swallows the steak and looks at me. He points with the knife. "Who is this?"

"This is my son," Jack says before I can answer.

"Truth?" El Chacal says. He looks closer. "Yes. I see it now. It's in the eyes. He has your eyes." He taps his temple with his knife. "The eyes always give the man away. There's no hiding what's in the eyes."

Back to Esteban. "You stole from me."

Esteban shakes even harder. He looks like he's going to collapse on the spot. "No, *jefe*, no. I would never steal from you."

El Chacal saws off another piece and stuffs it in his mouth. "People who steal from me make me very angry. You know what happens to them?"

The brothers take hold of Esteban's arms. He hangs there. Tears start to run down his face. "Please don't kill me. I'll do anything."

El Chacal laughs. It's more of a bark than a laugh. It makes me think of a wild dog. "I'm not going to kill you, Esteban."

Esteban lifts his head. "You're…not?"

El Chacal swallows. "No. If I kill you, you can't pay me back the money you stole."

"Thank you, thank you," Esteban babbles. "I'll pay you every *sol*. You can count on me. Can…can I go now?"

"Yes. But wait one moment. There is one thing first." El Chacal looks at me. "Did Jack tell you about my pets?" I shake my head. "Come closer. You want to see this."

I glance at Jack, then take a couple of steps forward. Jack does too. I notice that Esteban has gone very still. I wonder what these pets are that El Chacal is talking about. Some kind of dogs most likely.

El Chacal saws off another piece of steak, but instead of putting it in his mouth, he tosses it into the pool.

Instantly the surface of the pool begins to boil. I catch glimpses of fish scales and fins.

And teeth. Lots and lots of teeth.

The steak is gone in seconds. Esteban moans and starts thrashing. But the brothers have their meat hooks on him and he's not going anywhere.

"They are small, but fierce," El Chacal says, a big smile on his face. "One by itself is not so much, but when there are many of them…" His eyes light up.

"Don't do this!" Esteban wails. "I beg you, please, please…"

El Chacal nods to the brothers.

Esteban fights, but he's got no chance. Chato and Gordo force him to his knees. It's hard to stand there and watch. I want to do something. I look at my father. He gives a small shake of his head.

Chato holds Esteban in place, while Gordo takes hold of his left forearm. He forces Esteban's hand down toward the water until it's almost touching.

"Halt!" El Chacal says.

Gordo stops. Esteban looks up hopefully. Tears streak his face.

El Chacal tosses Gordo the steak knife. "It has to be bloody. It's better that way."

Gordo slices the back of Esteban's hand and shoves it into the water.

The piranhas swarm around Esteban's hand. He begins screaming. I grit my teeth and look away.

It seems like forever until it is done. Gordo pulls Esteban's hand from the water. It is no longer the hand of a man. It is the hand of a skeleton. The flesh is gone. Only the bones and shreds of tendon remain. I feel a strong urge to throw up.

"Wrap that up," El Chacal says. "He can't pay me if he bleeds to death."

Chato hauls the weeping man away. Gordo remains there, arms crossed, watching us. From his expression there is no way to tell that he just held a man's arm while fish ate his hand.

"They're called piranhas," El Chacal says. "The Indians say they can strip a horse to the bone in under five minutes. I have not tested this myself yet, but I can say this from personal experience: it takes less than four minutes for them to devour a man."

There's not much to say to that. I know that's something I hope I never see.

Two servants come out of a door and walk over to the table. One is an old woman with her gray hair tied up in a bun. The other is a young girl, probably about twelve, her long, black hair braided. They are both dressed in servants' uniforms, black dresses with white, lacy aprons over them. The old woman is carrying a silver tray with a coffee pot and a cup on it.

The young girl gathers up El Chacal's plate and silverware. The old woman sets the tray down and pours a cup of coffee.

El Chacal brushes crumbs from his coat and turns toward us. He looks me up and down, then looks at my father. "Is he like you, I wonder?"

"More than he wants to admit."

"Hopefully with better judgment than you."

"I don't know yet. We've spent most of the time arguing so far."

El Chacal looks at me again. "Your father has quite the love of gambling."

"Tell me something I don't know," I say.

"He has been on a losing streak, and now he owes me a great deal of money. I am starting to become angry with him."

Chato returns. He stands behind my father.

"Give me a week," Jack says. "I'll have it for you."

El Chacal ignores him. He picks up his coffee cup and takes a sip.

Instantly he spits it out. "It's not hot enough!" he screams at the old woman. "I told you I want it hot! How stupid are you?" He throws the rest of the coffee on the front of her dress.

The old woman stands unmoving, her face impassive. He slams the cup down. She takes the cup and the pot and walks away, followed by the girl.

El Chacal looks at Jack again. He smiles. It's a wolf's smile.

"One week. And an extra one thousand *sols*."

"That's not fair," Jack says.

"Do you think the piranhas care what is fair, Jack?" he asks. "No. They only want to eat. One week. Every sol. Or I will find out how long it takes my little pets to eat you."

Chapter 14

The coach takes us back to the restaurant. It doesn't stop. When we get close, Chato opens the doors and Gordo tosses us out like stray dogs. Jack dusts himself off and looks after them.

"That didn't go so bad."

"We saw a man get his hand eaten by fish," I say. "And El Chacal said he would feed you to those same fish in a week. How is that not bad?"

"I've seen worse, believe me."

He starts for his horse, but I stop him. "Why?"

He raises an eyebrow.

"Why did you do it? Why borrow money from someone like that?"

"I thought I was going to win."

"That's not an answer."

He frowns, thinking. "I'm not sure how to explain it."

"Try."

"There's a feeling I get when I'm gambling. Nothing else compares. Not liquor. Not women. Nothing in the whole world. When I am gambling, I know that I am alive."

"It sounds like you won't be much longer."

"You see now why I called you down here, why this map is so important," he says. "I must pay him or die."

"Why not give him the map?" I ask.

For the first time Jack seems upset. "Are you crazy? *Give* him the map?"

"Why not? Better than being eaten by piranhas."

"Even supposing he does not simply take it and still force me to pay, that is a terrible idea."

"Why?"

"Because this map is my big chance. It's the opportunity I've been looking for my whole life," he says.

"It won't do you any good if you're dead."

"I don't intend to be dead. What's wrong with you, Ace? What happened to you?"

"What are you talking about?"

"You're too young to be so old. Where's your sense of adventure?"

I think about the Aztec god Totec coming to life. I think about the things on the ghost ship. "Adventures aren't as much fun as you think."

He shakes his head. "I'm disappointed in you. Because this, this is the chance of a lifetime. This is a chance few men ever get and even fewer have the courage to take."

"Is everything about money to you?"

He throws his hands up. "Haven't you been listening to me at all? It's not about the money. It's never been about the money. The money is nice, sure. I like to spend as much as anyone. But it's not about that. If it was simply about the money, I'd rob banks or something. No, this is about the *thrill*. It's about the excitement. It's about being alive."

"Even if it kills you."

"Even if it kills me."

I stare at him in disbelief. Then I shake my head and turn away. "I'm done. You do whatever you want." I take up Coyote's reins.

"Where are you going?" Jack asks.

"I don't know." I really don't. Talking to him has me rattled. Or maybe it was seeing a man get his hand eaten. Whichever. All I know is that when I'm around this man my thinking gets twisted up.

He puts his hand on my shoulder. "Hold on. Don't run off. It's getting late. Where are you going to stay tonight?"

"I haven't figured that out yet. I've been a little busy, what with getting shot at and threatened with fish."

"Come with me then. We'll get a room in the old part of the city. You'll like it. It's pretty. I know a great place to eat. We can sit and talk. You can tell me what you've been doing with your life," he says.

I'm suspicious. I'm angry. But I'm also hungry and tired. So I hesitate.

"Come on. It can't hurt to spend a few hours with your old man, can it?"

"A few hours with you today almost got me killed, what, two times? Three?"

"You're exaggerating. You weren't in any danger from El Chacal. He has no beef with you."

"He's a mad dog. There's no telling what he'll do."

"I will answer any question you ask," he says.

"The truth?" I say.

"The truth."

I don't believe him. I still don't get on my horse, though. Every instinct tells me I should. I should climb on Coyote and ride away without looking back. Nothing good can come from being around Jack.

He grins. "It's settled then. Let's go get some grub." He goes and gets on his horse and starts down the street. I stare after him for a few moments, then mount up and follow him.

I'm going to regret this.

An hour later the horses are stabled and we're sitting on a balcony overlooking Lima's grand plaza in the old part of the city. This part of the city is a lot different from what I've seen so far. The buildings are huge and old, the walls made of thick adobe. The doors and shutters are ornately carved from some wood that so dark it's almost black.

The plaza is large and very clean. It is bordered by tall stone buildings. On one side is a huge Catholic church with twin bell towers. The middle of the plaza is a park teeming with lush flowers and old trees whose limbs sweep the ground. Young couples walk hand-in-hand around the plaza, while the old men and women look on from benches.

"The Spaniards built this part of the city," my father says. "They were bastards all right, but they knew how to build."

"You said I could have answers," I say. The waiter comes and sets tall glasses in front of us.

"I did. Ask. I'll tell you anything you want to know."

"Where did you get the map?"

"I stole it." He blinks like he's surprised. "Hey, that wasn't as hard as I thought it would be."

"I know you stole it. That doesn't tell me anything. Who did you steal it from?"

He holds up one finger. "Not who. Where."

"Where?"

"From a museum."

"What's that?"

"It's a place where they keep old things."

That makes no sense to me. "Old things? Why?"

"So people can go look at them."

Now I'm even more confused. If things are still good, use them. If they're no good, throw them away. Why keep them just to look at? But I don't want to get sidetracked, so I say, "Whose museum? I want to know who else is going to pop up and try and kill me."

He grins. "You have nothing to worry about. No one even knows it's gone. It was hidden in a secret drawer in an old chest. They didn't even know they had it."

"Who is 'they'?"

He shrugs. "The government. It's not much of a museum, just a bunch of old stuff in a warehouse on the edge of the city. Hardly anyone goes there."

That all sounds a little too convenient to me. There's something he's not telling me. I can feel it. "How did you find out about it?"

"I met an old man—"

"The truth."

He gets a hurt look that I don't believe for a second. "This *is* the truth. I met an old man one night. He looked lonely. I sat down and bought him a drink. We stayed up the whole night. He was a fascinating man. I don't know if it was the drink or if he saw something in me he liked, but around dawn he told me about the map. He said he'd go get the treasure himself, but he was too old. I thought he was crazy. I said goodbye and walked away laughing. But I kept thinking about it. Finally, I had to go look for myself."

Something is fishy about his story. "You said no one knows the map is gone. But earlier you said you had to mail it to me because you were in trouble."

"Okay. I misled you a little. *Almost* no one knows about it."

"Do you ever stop lying?"

"I just…I didn't want to upset you anymore than you already are. It was the night watchman at the museum. He found me while I was retrieving the map. I paid him a bribe to look the other way. A good one too. But then he got greedy and gathered up some friends. They came after me. But we don't need to worry about them."

"Why's that?"

"Because I said so. Can't you just trust me?"

"That's the problem. I don't. You lied to get me into this. How do I know you're not still lying? Everything you say is a lie. And now I'm stuck in this country. I'm out of money and I've got no way to get home."

He makes this little sad sound. "It's not all lies. I am in deep trouble. You met El Chacal. You saw what he's capable of."

An image comes to me of the man getting his hand chewed up. That's something I won't forget right away. Or ever.

"But you're right about one thing. I had no right to rope you into this. This isn't your problem, it's mine." He sits up straighter. "I got into it, and I'll get out of it. I'm going to fix this. We'll go down to the docks tomorrow morning. Don't worry. I'll get you home."

"Coyote too."

He winces. "That's not going to make this easier."

"Either Coyote goes, or I don't go."

He nods. "I'll get him on the ship too. I don't know how, but I'll do it." He takes a drink and looks off into the distance, thinking.

Down on the plaza a man takes a seat underneath a flowering tree. He has a guitar slung over his shoulder. He tunes it for a minute, then begins playing. It's a sad, haunting song. He starts to sing. I don't understand the words, but they fill me with a strange sadness.

We sit there in silence, listening. I look at my father, really look at him for the first time. There are lines on his face. They're deeper than I realized. There's gray in his hair that I didn't see either. It hits me then. My father is getting old.

"Maybe I could put off leaving for a little while," I say. "Help you out some."

"No. You were right. I caused this problem and I need to fix it. I've already dragged you through too much. I won't involve you anymore."

When the song is over, my father stands up. He looks down at me. "I'm sorry. About saying I was disappointed in you. I'm not. I'm proud of you, Ace. I'm proud of the man you've become.

I've been thinking about you a lot lately for some reason. I realize now that I sent you the map and the telegram because I wanted to see you. I wanted to do this with you, to have one thing that was just the two of us. I'm sorry."

With that he walks away, leaving me sitting there with my thoughts. I'm confused. It's like there are two men who call themselves my father, and I don't know which one is the true one. There's the one who left without saying goodbye, who lied to get me down here to help him. And then there's the one I just saw.

Which one is real?

Chapter 15

In the morning Jack is cheerful. It's like the night before never happened. He gets up from his bed and goes to the window and looks out.

"It's going to be a great day," he says. "Look at that sky. Not a cloud anywhere." He turns to me. "Let's go find you a ship."

He talks rapidly while I'm getting dressed and gathering my gear. I don't have much to say back. The truth is, I'm feeling bad about leaving him here. It doesn't make any sense to me. Why should I feel bad? I'm not the one who told him to get into debt with El Chacal. I'm not the one who lied to get me down here.

It's all true, but it doesn't make me feel better. I feel kind of awful, actually.

Finally, I say, "Why don't you come too? Get out of Lima. El Chacal is a big deal down here, but the United States is a long way away."

"No. It's time I quit beating the devil around the stump. I did this. I need to own up to it."

"That's good but getting yourself killed over it is stupid, if you ask me."

He whacks me on the arm. "Then I'll just have to make sure I don't get myself killed. Don't cash in my chips too fast. I've still got an ace up my sleeve." He winks when he says this, making sure I get his little joke.

"Come on. We don't want to dally. High tide is coming."

At the stable, I put a bridle on Coyote, then turn away to pick up my saddle. I turn back to see Jack reaching for Coyote's head.

"Don't do that!" I say.

"Do what?" he says.

"Don't touch Coyote's head. Don't touch him anywhere."

"Why not?"

"Coyote doesn't like being touched. He's liable to take your finger off."

"Aw, I don't believe that." And then he goes and scratches Coyote behind the ear.

I suck in a breath, sure I'm about to see him down a finger or two.

But Coyote doesn't bite him. I can't believe my eyes. He even looks like he likes it, lowering his head and closing his eyes a little bit.

"You're just a big pussy cat, aren't you?" Jack says, scratching behind the other ear. He looks at me with a big smile. "You love to exaggerate, don't you?"

I don't know what to say. The only thing Coyote likes better than biting people is kicking them. I feel kind of betrayed, though it makes no sense to me.

"Usually he bites people who try to touch him," I say.

"Maybe you should try scratching him more," he says. "Animals are like people. They like it when you're nice to them."

Now I feel grumpy. "You don't know what you're talking about. You don't know what we've been through."

"Sure. Only think about it, okay? You catch more flies with honey than vinegar, you know." He gives Coyote a last pat and goes to his horse.

I've never understood that saying. Why would anyone want to catch flies, anyway? I mutter something under my breath and toss my saddle on Coyote's back. While I'm tightening the cinch, in a low voice I say to Coyote, "Thanks a lot for that, traitor."

Coyote peels his lips back and tosses his head. I know he's laughing at me.

"You did that on purpose, didn't you?" I say.

He sneezes, blowing snot all over me. Sometimes I hate him.

We ride out of the stable. We're crossing the plaza when Jack suddenly says, "Uh oh." He pulls his hat down and turns his face away.

"What is it? What's wrong?" I'm looking around, but I don't see anyone pointing a gun at us.

He motions with his chin. "Over there."

I follow the motion and see two soldiers on foot by one of the streets. They've stopped a man and are asking him questions.

"All I see are two soldiers. That doesn't—" I break off as a growing suspicion takes hold of me. "Is the army after you too?"

"No, no. Of course not." Meanwhile, he's riding the other way. I follow after.

"If they're not after you, then why are you running?"

"I'm not running," he says, shooting a look back over his shoulder. "I'm being smart. If you'd been here as long as I have, you'd do the same."

We take another street. Once the soldiers are out of sight, he relaxes and pushes his hat back.

"You don't know about the Colonel yet," he says.

"Sure I do. He's the only one in this city hasn't shot at me," I say. "Yet."

Jack ignores that. "People think it's the president that runs this country. But Menendez is nothing. He gives speeches and waves to crowds. Colonel Guzman is the one who really runs things."

I'm still suspicious. "What does that have to do with you?"

"It's not me. It's all foreigners. The Colonel hates them all. Now and then he rounds up however many he can get his hands on. Then it's a quick trial and a firing squad."

Once more on the way to the docks we have to change our route to avoid soldiers at an intersection. I can see it's got Jack touchy. He doesn't talk much and keeps his eyes moving, watching for them.

We make it down to the docks okay and ride along them. "The man I know is a mate on that ship at the end," Jack says. "I think they're getting ready to put out in the next couple of days. They might be able to take you on, if you're willing to work."

"I had to work to get down here," I say, thinking about all the hours I spent mopping and scrubbing.

Before we can get there, I hear a commotion behind us. We look back and see a whole squad of mounted soldiers coming down the street. At their head is a man on horseback wearing a black hat and a long, black coat.

"Shit," Jack says. "That's him. Stay calm. They might not notice us."

A shout from behind us, ordering us to halt.

"Keep going," Jack says. "Act like you didn't hear. We can go into that alley right there."

We keep riding. I feel like there's a target on my back. It's hard to keep walking.

Another shout. Then a gunshot.

"Go!" Jack yells.

We take off running. The pounding of hooves behind us as the soldiers give chase. We turn down a narrow alley between low buildings with flat roofs. The alley ends after a few hundred feet, boxed in by the back side of a crumbling building and a rotting, wooden fence.

Jack doesn't hesitate. He bends low over the neck of his horse and spurs her straight at the fence. She gathers herself and jumps over it. Coyote and I are right behind. More shots fly by.

We charge across a small open space filled with dead weeds and cut between two houses. Children scatter out of the way. We duck under a clothesline. I don't duck far enough and end up with a dress wrapped around my head.

We go over a pile of rubble and charge through some brush. There aren't any houses or buildings here, only open country. We ride up a steep embankment and onto a small path worn through the undergrowth. The path leads us into a patch of thick trees.

A few yards into the trees, he leads us off the path. We duck under some low-hanging limbs and stop.

"Quiet now," he whispers.

Through the trees I can just see the soldiers as they ride past on the path. The Colonel isn't with them. They're moving fast, not even looking around. In a minute we can no longer hear them.

"That was close," Jack says. We go back to the path and go the other way.

"Closer than I'd like," I say. "Are you sure they're not after you?"

"Why would they be after me?"

"I don't know. Maybe because you stole a treasure map from them?"

"The Colonel doesn't know anything about this map, I promise you."

I don't say anything.

"You don't believe me, do you?"

"I didn't say I don't believe you."

"We can talk about it later. Right now we need to get off the streets."

"We're off right now, aren't we?" I say.

"Very funny. You know what I mean."

We follow the path back to the edge of the city and ride down a narrow, winding street that takes us back up onto the bluffs where most of the city is located.

"I know a place where we can keep our heads down while we figure out what to do next," he says. "It's right around the corner."

We stop in front of a wooden building with a sign on the front that says "Drink" in faded paint. Simple and to the point. I like that. We climb down off our horses and are heading for the door when a familiar figure comes around the corner of the building and points a gun at us.

Chapter 16

It's Myron, the short one with the freckles. He's grinning ear to ear.

"I told Lonnie you'd come here," he says. "He argued with me, but I was right. It's like my grandma used to tell me, 'snakes always go back to their hole.'"

A man comes to the door of the building, sees what's going on, spins on his heel and heads straight back inside.

"Lonnie!" Myron calls over his shoulder.

He's careful not to take his eyes off us. Which is too bad. All I need is a split second. I work my fingers a little, make sure they're loose.

"Get up here! I caught 'em! Damn it, where the hell are you? It shouldn't take that long to take a piss, even for you." Under his breath he adds, "That man pees more than anyone I ever saw. Like a damned pregnant sow."

Jack turns his head then, like he's looking at someone over Myron's shoulder. There's no one there. He smiles. "You picked the perfect time to show up, Joe. Shoot this man for me, will you?"

"What?" Myron says. "There ain't anyone behind me. You're just saying that to get me to look. Lonnie!"

"Shoot him and I'll cut you in on the treasure," Jack says.

Myron can't help it. He turns his head.

That's all the opening I need.

My gun flashes into my hand. I squeeze the trigger.

A puff of smoke and Myron's gun goes flying out of his hand. "Ow!" he yells, holding his hand. "What'd you go and do that for?"

"I could have put that bullet in your liver," I say. "Isn't this better?"

"Go on, Myron," Jack says. "Get out of here."

64

Still holding his hand, Myron backs away. "You ain't seen the last of us, Jack. We're gonna get that map." He turns and runs off, still yelling for Lonnie.

"You're fast," Jack says.

I drop my gun back in its holster and follow Jack inside. The place is dim and dusty. A handful of men sit at tables talking in low voices. Eyes turn to us, then move away. In a niche in the wall is a crucifix, the stub of a candle burning at its base.

We sit down at an empty table. A man comes by in a stained apron. He sets a bottle and two chipped cups down in front of us. Jack hands him a coin and he leaves without saying anything.

"Emilio is deaf," Jack says. "That makes him the perfect bartender. You never have to worry about him spreading any of your secrets around."

"It's time for the truth," I say.

"About what? I've told you everything."

"About Myron and Lonnie. Those aren't just two criminals trying to steal the map from you. Who are they really?"

Jack pours himself some of whatever is in the bottle and takes a drink. He makes a face and coughs a little. "I don't know what he makes this stuff out of, but if you ask me, Emilio is the real criminal here. Gah, this stuff is awful."

"Stop ducking the question."

"Okay, okay. I might not have been completely truthful with you about them."

"Or about anything."

"That's not fair."

"A man I knew used to say a fair is where you take your pigs to be judged," I say. I'm talking about Jack. He used to say that when I'd complain he wasn't being fair when we played cards.

Jack laughs. "I remember that. It used to make you so mad."

"I still don't know what it means."

"Well, a fair is a big gathering where the farmers from miles around bring their pigs and such—"

"You're ducking the question again."

"So I am." He takes another drink and pounds the table.

"If it's so bad, why do you keep drinking it?"

"I don't want to hurt Emilio's feelings." He pours me some. I push the cup away. "All right," he says. "Here's the truth. I hired them to help me steal the map."

"And then you cheated them."

"That hurts, Ace. And it's not true. I paid them, but it wasn't enough. They tried to dry gulch me, but I got away. But they're not giving up."

"Is that really what happened?"

He holds a hand up. "I swear."

"Big deal."

He gets a twinkle in his eye. He takes a deck of cards out of his pocket and lays them on the table. Puts his hand on them and repeats, "I swear."

I guess I'll take that. A deck of cards is basically a Bible for Jack.

Chapter 17

We spend the rest of the day there, keeping our heads down. Every now and then Jack goes to the room's lone window and stares out for a few minutes. I ask him if he's not worried about Myron and Lonnie coming in and trying to get him.

"No," he says. "They know they're not welcome here anymore. Emilio will pepper their hides if they so much as put a toe through that door."

"What did they do to make Emilio so angry at them?"

"Myron drank some of his homemade liquor and called it cat piss. Emilio is very sensitive about his booze."

In a low voice I say, "I think calling it cat piss is being generous." I was dumb enough to take a drink a few minutes ago.

"Shh. You don't want Emilio to hear you."

I remember something he said then. "I thought you said he's deaf."

"He is."

"Then how...?"

He shrugs. "I don't know. He just does."

I figure he's pulling my leg, but when I turn and look, I see Emilio standing there glaring at me. I give him a little wave. His expression never changes. I smile and take a big drink, then rub my stomach like I love the taste. He turns away and goes into the back room.

I don't feel so good after that. "Can we get anything to eat here?" I ask Jack.

"The sign says 'Drink.' It doesn't say anything about eating, does it?"

He's got me there.

He takes the deck out again and starts shuffling it. "How about we play some cards to pass the time?"

"I don't have any money."

"That's okay. I can loan you some."

"I already know you're going to cheat."

"I'll tell you what. Any hand you catch me cheating, you win. Is that fair enough?"

"I don't want to play cards."

"Sure you do. Come on. I'm going crazy sitting here."

"No."

"Fine." He stands up. "I'll go see if any of these other gentlemen want to play."

I can already see where this will go. I picture lots of shouting and shooting. I sigh. "You win. I'll play."

"I knew you'd change your mind. Draw or stud?"

"I don't care."

"Draw it is." He starts dealing. It's impressive, I have to admit that. His hands move so fast it's hard to follow them. The cards fly out like bullets. I watch as close as I can, but I still have a feeling I'm missing something.

He finishes dealing and fishes some money out of his pocket. "Here, I'll front you a hundred *sols*. You can pay me back out of your share of the treasure."

"There won't be any share for me. I'm not going on any fool treasure hunt," I say.

"You say that now…"

"I'll say it later too." I pick up my cards. "How much is a hundred *sols*? Is it a lot?"

"It's like a peso, only smaller."

Yeah, that tells me a lot. I'm looking at a pair of tens. I pick up a coin and peer at it. I think it's worth one sol. I toss it into the pot. "One sol."

"One sol? Come on, Ace. Did you lose your big boy pants?"

"I told you I don't even know what a sol is worth!"

"Okay, kiddie poker it is then."

I throw my cards down on the table. "I'm out."

"Come on, Ace. Lighten up. I was only joshing. You need to lighten up. You're too tense."

That makes me mad, but it also makes me wonder. Is he right? Maybe I'm being too hard on him. I have been riding him pretty hard since I got here. I take another sip of my drink. It's not quite as bad as it was. I think I'm getting used to it.

I pick up my cards. "You want to play? Let's play." I throw twenty sols in the pot.

Jack grins and rubs his hands together. "That's more like it."

We go at it then. He calls me. I keep the tens and an ace kicker. A third ten comes up in the draw. He draws three cards. I throw another fifty sols in the pot. He raises. I raise. He calls. I show my tens. He throws down three jacks.

"You cheated," I say.

He leans forward. His eyes are lit up. "Maybe I did."

"Then I win. You said—"

He stops me when I reach for the pot. "How? How did I cheat?"

He's got me there. "I don't know."

"Then you don't know if I really cheated. It could be just luck. Don't be a sore loser." He rakes in his winnings and chuckles.

I know why so many people want to shoot him.

I take another sip and pick up the cards. I actually have a deck I carry around with me. I practice with it sometimes when I'm bored. I let my hands take over and try not to think. "Enjoy it while it lasts, pale face, because that's the last hand you're going to win," I say.

"Pale face? Really?"

"Maybe you like cheating skunk better?" I say. I'm goading him, trying to get him to listen to what I'm saying and not pay so much attention to what I'm doing. I see an ace flash and slip it to the bottom of the deck.

"Pale face is better," he says. "More a description than an insult."

"Trust me. It's an insult." While I'm talking, I'm dealing. On the last card I slide the ace out and into my hand.

Jack shakes his head. "Come on, Ace. You can do better than that."

"What are you talking about? I thought we were here to play cards."

"I saw you bottom deal that ace to yourself. I saw you put it there when you were insulting me."

"No, you didn't."

"Don't be sulky. You learned everything you know from me, remember?"

He's right, but that doesn't mean that I like it. I gather up the cards and reshuffle. I play it straight this time.

"It was well done, though. Not many would have noticed it," he says. He chuckles. That makes me mad.

We settle in for some serious cards then. I want to beat him so bad I can taste it. And I do. Sometimes. I catch him with a card in his sleeve. I bluff him once and take a nice pot with a pair of deuces. The high point of the game is when I slip a Tennessee shuffle past him when he's refilling his cup. He bets hard on the straight I deal him, and I beat him with a flush.

But mostly I lose. My initial stake trickles away and he spots me another hundred. When that's gone, I go for five hundred. It takes longer to dribble away, but it goes all the same. He's just too good. I watch as close as I can, but he still manages to slip tricks by me.

At some point I realize we have an audience. Most everyone in the place is standing around us in a ring, watching. Even Emilio is there. He sets another bottle down and scoops up a coin. I wonder what happened to the first one. I don't recall having very much of it.

"Is good, no?" he says.

"It's the best," I reply. The next drink makes me cough.

I lose some more. The winning hands are getting harder to come by. I run out of money again.

"Another five hundred," I say.

But Jack puts the cards in his pocket. "You're already into me for fifteen hundred sols. Don't you think that's enough?"

"I don't even know how much that is. What can you buy with that? A plate a beans? A horse?"

"Somewhere between one and the other." He stands up and stretches. "I need to piss." As he turns, one of the men who's been watching suddenly punches him in the jaw. He staggers back, rubbing his jaw.

I leap out of my chair and throw myself at the man. He's short, heavyset, with a thick beard and a missing tooth. He smiles broadly as I punch him.

Just like that we're in a brawl. Someone breaks a chair across my back. I bloody his mouth. Jack kicks another man in the shin and then goes down under another man who bull rushes him. Even Emilio gets into the act, smashing an empty bottle over the head of a tall man with no shirt.

It fades out after a few minutes. I wipe blood off my chin, find an unbroken chair and sit down. My father pulls up a chair next to me. He's holding his ribs. He stands up a table, finds an unbroken bottle on the floor and picks it up. He takes a drink and passes it to me.

After I drink, I feel a tap on my shoulder. The heavyset man with the missing tooth is standing there, smiling. It looks like he's missing another tooth now. He motions for the bottle. I hand it to him.

He takes a drink and sits down next to us, passes the bottle to Jack.

"You throw a good punch," he says to me.

"What the hell?" I say. "Why did you punch Jack?"

He puts up his hands. "It's a *cantina*," he says. As if that explains anything.

"You're a real sonofabitch, you know that, Jose?" Jack says to him.

"You know this man?" I ask.

"Sure. We're old friends."

"Who sometimes get into bar fights for fun."

Jack takes a drink off the bottle and hands it to me. "Don't overthink it, Ace. It's a saloon."

Everyone laughs like he said the funniest thing ever. I give up trying to make sense of it and take a drink. Things stopped making sense when I got off the ship yesterday.

"Emilio!" Jack yells. "More of your finest! I'm paying!"

Emilio brings out an armload of bottles that taste even worse than the ones before. There's a lot of singing and yelling. At some point things die down and Jack says it's time to go. We say a lot of goodbyes and stumble outside. I'm surprised to see that it's almost dark.

"What happened to the day?" I say.

"Saloon time," Jack says very seriously.

I laugh like that's actually funny. "What now?"

"I don't think we can go to a hotel. It's too easy to find us there," he says. "I have just the place."

Chapter 18

We turn onto a narrow street that leads downhill. "I know some people who will put us up," Jack says.

We're on the south side of the city. The streets get narrower and dirtier as we go. The houses are little more than bits of wood with thatch roofs, all leaning against each other like they're about to fall down. Now and then there's one made of brick or stone, but not many. A pack of dogs, so skinny their ribs are like slats in a picket fence, go trotting by. They give us a yellow-eyed look. A man leans against the front of one of the houses, cradling a clay jug to his chest. His eyes track us as we pass by.

The sun is sliding to the horizon. Shadows gather. At the intersection ahead a half dozen young men are standing in a loose cluster. One has an ancient black-powder rifle strapped to his back. All of them have machetes slung from their belts. They stop talking and stare at us.

We go deeper into the slums. The streets are barely wide enough for us to ride side by side in most places. I see a dead cat nailed to a wall, limbs splayed. Is it a warning?

"A lot of unfriendly types around here," I say. "You sure it's a good idea to stay here?"

"We're not staying here," Jack says. "I don't know this barrio. We're heading for Barrio Mariposa."

"I hope you know what you're doing."

He flashes a smile. "Me too."

Ahead the street chokes down to only a few feet wide. There's a cart blocking the way. Two men are leaning up against it. One has no shirt. His beard goes down to his chest. The other has a red piece of cloth tied around his forehead. Both are wearing bandoliers strung over their shoulders, heavy pistols hanging from their hips. They scowl at us.

We stop in front of them. I slip my duster back so I can get to my pistols. I have a feeling this is about to turn bad. I hope we don't have to fight our way out of here. We took so many turns.

I'm not sure I can find my way out of here and it's going to be dark soon.

"Raul," my father says.

"Jack," the bearded man replies.

The moment drags out. My hands move closer to my guns.

Then Raul's bearded face splits in a smile. "It's good to see you again, *amigo*." He steps forward and reaches up. He and my father clasp hands. He looks at me.

"Who is this?"

"This is my son, Ace. Ace, this unruly looking fellow is Raul."

"You didn't say you have a son, Jack," Raul cries. He steps over to shake my hand. Naturally, Coyote goes for him. I yank on the reins, but Coyote still manages to nip him. The other man laughs.

"Sorry about that. He's not a friendly sort," I say.

Raul isn't angry. He looks at Coyote and nods. "He is a fighter. There is no reason for sorry."

"We're looking for a place to hole up for the night," Jack says. "Can we stay here?"

Raul nods. "*Sí*, Jack." He looks at me. "Welcome to Barrio Mariposa." He turns back to Jack. "The city, she is fearful today. *Los soldados*, they are everywhere."

"I know. We had a run-in with them earlier. That's why we're here."

"You are a friend of Mariposa. You are always welcome here."

"I brought a present," Jack says, taking a bottle out of his saddlebag.

Raul smiles broadly. "You sing a beautiful song."

The other man moves the cart to the side. We pass through. Raul calls after us. "Don't drink the whole bottle without me, Jack. I don't want to cut you!" Both men laugh.

The street gets so narrow that I could easily touch the homes on either side. The roofs are low, and I have to be careful not to get poked in the eye.

After a bit the street opens up into a small plaza. A lone tree grows in the center of the plaza, by a well with a low stone wall around it. Children chase each other, yelling and laughing. There are a handful of people around. They nod and smile at Jack, who smiles back and calls out greetings.

A young woman emerges from one of the huts. She is carrying a baby in a sling.

"Hold on for a second," Jack says. He hops down and walks over to her. He takes something wrapped in cloth out of his pocket. She sees him coming and smiles. Curious, I move closer.

"I found some," Jack says, handing her a small, brown bottle.

"Thank you, señor," she says.

"The doc said two drops every morning and every night," he says. "It should clear up in a few days."

"You are too kind." There are tears in her eyes. "How can I thank you?"

He waves it off. "You already did. Don't worry about it."

He comes back over.

I'm surprised. I feel like I'm looking at a whole different person that I don't know at all.

"What was that about?" I ask.

"It was nothing. She asked me to pick something up for her is all."

"It's medicine, isn't it?"

"I don't want to talk about it." Someone calls his name and he turns.

"Olivia!" he cries, throwing out his arms.

I recognize Olivia right away. She's the woman from the docks who was being shaken down by one of El Chacal's thugs. She throws her arms around Jack and squeezes. She barely comes up to his chest.

"It's good you are here!" she says. "Tonight we celebrate Inti Raymi. You must join us."

"What is Inti Raymi?"

"Is an old festival from the time of the Incas," she says.

"I'm always happy to join a party."

She lets go of him and notices me for the first time.

"Who is the young, handsome man?" Her broad face creases in a big smile and she bats her eyelashes at me. I immediately like her.

"This is my son, Ace."

"You never said you have a son."

"Are you sure? I'm sure I talked about him. Maybe you weren't paying attention."

"Maybe you are a rascal, Jack." She holds out a hand to me. "Welcome to Barrio Mariposa."

I thank her and squeeze her hand lightly. She beams at me.

"I have something to help with the fiesta, Olivia," Jack says, and surprises me for the second time since we got here. He takes a wad of bills out of his pocket and hands them to her. "To help pay for food and drink."

Her eyes light up. "Señor Jack, this is so generous of you! I will send boys to buy more right away." She puts her fingers in her mouth, and whistles so loud it hurts my ears. It cuts right through the noise. Everyone stops talking and turns to her.

"Hey, *muchachos!*" she yells at a group of young men clustered at one corner. I recognize several of the youths we passed earlier. "*Vengan!*"

They come at a trot. Clearly she is someone to be listened to in this neighborhood. She speaks to them rapidly.

Olivia comes back over, a young boy following her. He looks to be about twelve. "This is my grandson, Pedro. He will show you where you can put your horses."

Pedro leads us to a small pen where we can put our horses. He slaps an old sow who is sleeping there until she gets up and waddles away, grunting, then chases away the chickens roosting in the corners.

We put the horses in the pen. Pedro looks at my guns with big eyes. "Are you a gunfighter?" He mimes drawing pistols and shooting.

"Not really," I say.

"He is," Jack says. "He is very famous in America."

"Don't tell the boy that," I say.

"He asked."

"It's not true," I tell the boy. "I only use them when I have to."

"All the *bandidos* are very frightened of him," Jack tells Pedro. "They faint when they see him coming."

"I want to be a gunfighter someday," Pedro says.

"No, you don't. People shoot at you. Any day someone shoots at you is a bad day."

He nods, but I don't think he believes me. He runs off.

"Why'd you tell him that?" I say to Jack.

"Kids need heroes," he says.

"Next time don't say anything."

"There's no pleasing you, is there?"

After that, Olivia sends us with an old woman who takes us into her home. There's a crude fire pit in the corner, and a rough table with clay bowls on it. A wooden cross hangs on the wall. On one side is a doorway with a threadbare blanket hanging down over it. She pulls the blanket back, rolls up the straw mat lying on the floor, then gestures for us to put our bedrolls in the room.

"No, we can't take your bedroom," Jack says. "We'll stay out here."

She puts her hands on her hips and frowns at him.

"I don't think we have any choice," Jack says.

We toss our bedrolls down and go back out to help prepare for the festival.

We're put to work stringing decorations around the plaza, brightly colored bits of cloth and small, wooden carvings tied to string. Candles set inside glass jars to protect them from the wind are set out.

Meanwhile, the men of the neighborhood begin to return from the day's labors and they pitch in and help. A fire is built in a pit and a piglet is set to roasting over it. The young men Maria sent to get supplies return, bringing chickens, rice, beans and kegs of liquor. The liquor is tapped and begins to flow. The chickens are plucked, stuffed and put over the fire. Pots are set over the fire and begin bubbling. Makeshift tables are set up.

Jack goes over to the well to get some water, but Olivia stops him. "It's dry," she says.

"When did that happen?"

"More than a month ago."

"Where do you get water?"

"We carry it from the river."

"That's a long way to carry water," Jack says. I remember seeing the river when my ship was putting in. It's south of the city, a good trek from here.

"It is what it is," Olivia says, holding up her hands.

Jack shakes his head. "It's too far."

"There is nothing we can do. A new well costs, and El Chacal, he does not leave us much."

76

"You leave it to me, Olivia," Jack says. "I'm going to get you the money for a new well."

"No, Jack. It is not your problem."

He sets his jaw. "If it's your problem, it's my problem."

I look at my father with new eyes. Who is he, really? Part of me wonders if he means it or if it is like so many other things in his life, a temporary thing soon forgotten in the excitement.

The musicians arrive. A man carrying a guitar, another with a flute. With them is a woman in a long, billowing dress, her hair done up on top of her head with ornately-carved wooden combs. The men play and she sings. People sing along. It's some language I don't recognize. Definitely not Spanish. Kids run shouting here and there. More drink flows.

The food starts appearing on the tables and people dig in. People begin dancing. Grandmothers dance with small children. Young women shyly dance with the young men. A pretty young woman with flashing eyes takes my arm and drags me out to dance, though I protest.

It grows late. The fiesta thins. The fires die down. I see my father sitting up against a building and go flop down beside him.

"That was quite a party," I say.

"It was."

We sit there in silence for a bit. Then I say, "It was generous of you to pay for so much of it."

"Oh, that." He does that little wave with his hand, shooing away flies that aren't there. "They need it more than I do."

"Uh...did you forget about El Chacal and his piranhas?"

"Nope."

"It's kind of important, don't you think?"

"That's a problem for tomorrow."

We sit there for a while longer. I have a lot to chew over.

"Do you really mean what you said? About paying for a new well?" I ask him.

"I do. These people have it hard enough. They shouldn't have to walk miles for water."

"Where are you going to get the money?"

He looks at me like I'm simple. "From the treasure."

"You don't have the treasure."

"I have a map."

"You have half a map."

"Something will come up. I'll find the other half."

"I still can't believe you'd give the treasure away."

He looks over at me. "You still don't get it, do you? You haven't been listening. This treasure, it's not about the money. It's about the thrill."

I stare at him, sorting it out. Then it hits me. "It's another gamble, isn't it?"

He nods. "Exactly. The biggest one ever."

I sit back, trying to absorb it all. Suddenly, things I thought I knew about my father don't make sense anymore. I have too many new pieces and I don't know where to put them. I feel dizzy, and it's not the liquor.

He really doesn't care about the money. To him it's only a byproduct, like the fat drippings when cooking meat. He's not the selfish man I thought he was. He does care about others. He steps on them sometimes, but it's not out of malice.

"I was talking to a man earlier," he says, interrupting my thoughts. "He works down at the docks. He thinks he has a way to get you past the soldiers and onto a ship. He can get your horse on too. He says there is a ship sailing tomorrow afternoon for California. You can be on it."

I open my mouth. Part of me is screaming at me to shut up, that I'm a durned fool. But I blurt out the words anyway.

"No. I'm going with you. We're going to find the Heart of the Empire."

Chapter 19

"Señores! Wake up! You have to go. *Los soldados*!"

It's Pedro, Olivia's grandson, who showed us where to stable our horses. In the gray light of predawn, I can see that his eyes are very wide.

I get up and buckle on my gun belt. Jack is only a second behind me. He grabs his hat and clamps it down on his head.

"How long?" he asks Pedro.

"Not long. Five minutes maybe. Hurry."

We grab our gear and hurry out of the old woman's hut. The air is cold. The sun is about to come up. Olivia comes hurrying toward us.

"It is the Colonel!" she cries. "You must go! Quickly now! We will try to slow him down."

Our horses are brought to us. They've already been saddled. I wonder if the one who saddled Coyote got kicked very many times. Maybe Coyote didn't kick him at all. He's got his head up, ears perked as he listens to something I can't hear yet. He senses danger.

"That way," Olivia says, pointing down one of the narrow streets that leads away from the plaza. "Turn right at the end. Others will show you where to go then."

"We're much obliged, Olivia," Jack says, tipping his hat.

Obliged doesn't cover it. I can't believe these people are taking this risk for us. If they anger the Colonel, things will go very bad for them. They could just stand aside and do nothing. It would be a lot safer.

Jack swears suddenly and starts looking around.

"What is it?" I ask.

"My coat. I don't know where it is."

"Leave it. We can get you another one."

"No, we can't. The map is in the pocket."

"I know where it is," Pedro says, and takes off running, Jack right behind him.

I hear shouts, getting closer. I mount up and move to where I can see.

Down the street that we came in through yesterday I can see soldiers, probably two dozen of them, heading toward us. But they aren't moving very fast. The lane is choked with men carrying boxes, crates, kegs, bundles of wood. Cursing, the soldiers crash into them, shoving them out of the way.

The men offer no resistance. They give every appearance of trying to get out of the way. But in their haste, many of them drop what they're carrying. Soldiers trip over boxes and stumble on pieces of wood. Two men carrying a barrel drop it. It rolls downhill, knocking a couple of the soldiers over.

Then I see him appear at the corner. The Colonel.

He's sitting astride a tall, black horse. His skin is very pale, almost ghostlike. His eyes meet mine. I can feel the intensity from here.

Almost deliberately, he draws a long-barreled pistol and points it at me.

For a fraction of a second, I don't react. I'm like a rabbit frozen by the wolf.

Then I snap out of it and grab iron. My pistol comes up, and I fire right as he sights down the barrel of his gun.

I deliberately miss. I'd like to shoot him, but he's obviously a big wheel in this country. Shooting him would probably bring down all kinds of heat we don't want.

His hat flies off. He flinches, throwing one arm up over his head, almost like the sunlight hurts him.

Jack comes back with his coat and we gallop out of there.

Chapter 20

"You still want to help find the treasure?" Jack asks.

We've slowed our horses to a walk and are making our way down a wide street. The street is crowded with early-morning traffic, people hurrying to start their days, carrying sacks and boxes, driving goats, shouting at stubborn donkeys. There's no sign of pursuit.

"I said I'm in. I meant it."

"I wanted to make sure it wasn't the drink talking," he says with a grin. "You wouldn't be the first person to say something while drunk and regret it later."

"I wasn't drunk."

"Oh, you were drunk. I saw you dancing." His eyes get wide. "Unless…is that how you *always* dance?"

"Hey, I'm not that bad."

"No, not at all," he says, his grin getting bigger. "Lots of chickens dance just like that. After they get their heads chopped off."

Now I feel irritated. He's good at angering me. "Can we talk about something else? Like what we're going to do now?"

"I think it's time to leave the city," he says.

"And go where?"

"To Machu Picchu."

"What's that?"

"It's some old Incan ruins way up in the Andes Mountains."

"You think those are the ruins that are drawn on the map?" I ask.

"I'm sure of it. There's nothing else it could be."

"How do you know the treasure is in the ruins?"

"Machu Picchu was a summer place for the Incan emperor and his family. Where else would he hide his treasure?"

Okay, that makes sense. "But we're missing half the map. The half that tells us where in the ruins the treasure is hidden. I'm betting the treasure isn't just lying around. It's going to be almost impossible to find without the rest of the map."

"So, we'll find the rest of the map," he says, like it's as easy as that.

"Which is…?"

He grins. I think he enjoys the plain craziness of this whole thing. "Somewhere."

"Somewhere?"

"Yep."

"As plans go, that one is mighty thin," I say.

"There's a few details to work out still."

"The rest of the map is a big detail."

"We'll find it. Don't you fret."

"How?"

He shrugs. "Luck."

"Luck?"

"That's what I said."

"That's not a plan. That's pure foolishness."

"I'm a gambler," he says, like that explains anything. "You can't be a gambler if you don't believe in luck."

"Luck and foolishness aren't the same things."

"Sometimes they are. Look, what other choice do we have? At the very least, we should get out of the city long enough for the heat to die down."

"What about El Chacal? You're running out of time."

"You let me worry about El Chacal. I'll come up with something. I always do."

I think of the piranhas and shudder. If someone was threatening to feed me to those things, I'd be a whole lot more worried.

"Let's head to a market and pick up some supplies for the road," Jack says.

"Hold on," I say. "One more thing." He looks at me. "I want to know the truth about the soldiers."

"I told you already."

"No. That wasn't the truth. I saw the Colonel, Jack. He wasn't there by accident. He's chasing you. I want to know why."

He gets a pained look on his face. "Do we have to do this right now?"

"Right now."

"Okay. You're right. He is chasing me. That museum I told you about? It wasn't a museum, not exactly."

"What was it?"

"It was kind of the Colonel's office."

"You stole the map from the Colonel?" I say loudly.

"Keep it down," he says, looking around to make sure no one heard. "Yes, I stole it from the Colonel."

"I've heard a lot of stupid things, Jack, but that has got to be the dumbest."

"Dumber than sneaking up on a giant grizzly bear?" he says with a sly look.

I knew I shouldn't have told the newspaper man about my run-in with Old Mose. "Dumber than that. A grizzly will give up after a while."

"Maybe not my smartest move," he admits. "But there's no need to get so worked up. That's your problem, Ace. You take every little thing and blow it up."

"Having the Peruvian army chasing us and shooting at us is not a little thing!" I say, realizing I'm getting close to shouting. "It's exactly the opposite of a little thing. It's a very, very large thing."

"That's good. Keep shouting. Why not shoot your gun in the air while you're at it? That should help them find us."

"No, no, no. You're not blaming this on me. This is your fault, not mine," I say.

"Does it really matter whose fault it is?"

"It does. It matters a lot. It says that one of us here can't be trusted. For anything."

"There you go, getting all excited again."

I put my head in my hands. "I can't believe you stole the map from the most powerful man in the country. Do you *want* to get killed?"

"That's a foolish thing to say. No, I don't want to get killed."

"Because it sure looks like it. Why else would someone want to anger someone who can send an *entire* army after them?"

"There's more to it than that."

"Oh good. I can't wait to hear it."

"Give it up, Ace. You don't do sarcasm well." He plucks at my coat sleeve. "Can you listen to me for a minute without shouting? Can you?"

"I'll think about it."

"Do you want to know why the Colonel is so hot to get his hands on that treasure?"

"I don't know. To buy himself something, I expect."

"He wants to overthrow the president."

"So?"

"I'm not finished. Once he does that, the first thing he'll do is invade Chile. That's what the treasure is for, to hire more soldiers, buy more guns. If he does that, think how many people will suffer. Thousands. Tens of thousands. That right there is plenty of reason to keep the treasure out of his hands."

I'm not buying it. I shake my head. "Do you really expect me to believe that's why you stole the map?"

"Maybe not the only reason. But it has a lot to do with it."

"Then why not destroy it? That way you can make sure no one gets it."

"Now, Ace. You're letting your anger talk for you. That's a foolish idea and you know it."

"There. See? I was right. You stole it for yourself, for the thrill of it. It's all a big game to you."

"That's some of it, sure. But that's not all of it."

"Why don't you just admit that you're chasing this treasure for you? You can make up whatever else you want to, but that's the reason, the real reason."

For the first time he looks mad. "It is for me. But not like you think. Since you're so damned set on it, I'll tell you what this is all about. This won't come as a big surprise to you, but I've never really done anything. What am I but a drifter and a gambler? The only thing I ever did that was worthwhile is father you, and even that is really all your mother's doing, not mine. This is my chance to do something with my life. This is my chance to make a mark before it's too late. I can stop something bad from happening, and I can use the money to do something good for people at the same time. It's a long shot, I'll grant that, but if the dice land right, I'll make up for everything else in one fell swoop."

He stops, breathing hard. I stare at him suspiciously, but I can't see any sign that he's conning me. He sure seems sincere.

"Is that really true?" I ask.

"Who cares? I'm tired of trying to convince you. You've already made up your mind about me. I can't change that. I'm going to find this treasure now, with or without you. You do whatever you want."

He twitches the reins and rides away without looking back.

I watch him go. I see that Coyote is looking at me. "Don't you judge me too," I tell him. "Why should I trust him? He's never done anything to earn that trust."

Coyote snorts and tosses his head.

"Don't tell me you believe him. How do you know he isn't just saying that to get me to help him?"

Coyote paws the ground.

"There are other cities, you know. Other places we could catch a ship home."

Coyote turns his face away.

"Okay, okay. You win. But when this all goes sideways, I'm blaming you."

I take off after my father.

I'm the world's biggest idiot.

Chapter 21

We've been out of Lima for a few days now. We're climbing up into the Andes Mountains, riding on a narrow, winding road late in the afternoon. We haven't seen any sign of the army following us. That means several days where no one has taken a shot at me. I could get used to this.

Where the road narrows down and crosses a stream, we come upon a peculiar sight. It's an old man leading a donkey. But that's not what's peculiar. What's peculiar is the old man is carrying a huge sack on his back—so big he's hard to see underneath it— while his donkey isn't carrying anything at all. Donkeys are ornery critters, and not good tasting, which means there's no earthly reason to have one except for carrying things.

Making things worse is that the donkey is being a donkey, which means stubborn. The creature is standing at the edge of the stream, all four hooves planted firmly, refusing to go another step. The old man is standing in the middle of the stream, a steady stream of wheedling coming from him.

Finally, the old man drops the donkey's lead rope, finishes crossing the stream, and throws his monstrous bundle down. He goes back, grabs the lead rope, and tries again. He really puts his all into it this time, huffing and puffing, throwing up water.

No luck. The donkey flattens her ears back and leans back on her haunches. For some reason that only makes sense to donkeys, and probably not even then, she refuses to take another step.

The old man loses it then. Cursing up a blue streak, he charges out of the stream and starts whacking the animal with the end of the lead rope.

Which makes no difference at all. The whole time the donkey stands there placidly. She doesn't so much as flinch. She lowers her head and crops some grass.

The old man gives up. He leans against the donkey and weeps. The donkey brings her head around and nips him on the shoulder. The old man jumps and hits her with his hat, which doesn't do anything except to make the hat fall apart faster.

"You need some help?" Jack asks him in Spanish.

The old man yelps and about jumps out of his skin. He must not have seen us there.

"She is a demon from hell," he replies in broken Spanish.

Jack holds out his hand. The old man hands him the lead rope. "Is no good, señor."

Jack spurs his mare. She crosses the stream. The donkey follows willingly.

That brings more cursing from the old man. I don't understand any of the words, since he's not speaking Spanish now, but he's really giving it his all. I'm impressed.

The sun is going down soon. There's a good spot to camp on the other side of the stream, a fire pit already built and some decent pieces of wood lying around. We pull our saddles and loose the horses to graze.

Jack asks the old man if he wants to join us and share our grub. The old man nods. He carries his monster sack over to the camp and drops it on the ground. He pulls the halter off the donkey and yells at her. The donkey stands there placidly, chewing on something, staring at him. The old man stomps over to the fire pit.

"You're not worried about your donkey running off?" Jack asks him.

"I am happy if she does," the old man grumbles and sits down. He is ancient, his hair pure white, the lines in his face deep and numerous. He's wearing loose wool pants and a shapeless cotton shirt. His straw hat is mostly pieces. His sandals are woven of some kind of fiber.

"I don't want to pry," Jack says, "but how come you carry all this—" He points at the huge sack. "—and the donkey carries nothing?"

"It is a big problem," the old man agrees. He shouts at the donkey, "Why you no carry anything, you old witch!"

The donkey throws her head and peels her lips back. It looks like she's laughing at the old man.

"She is *el diablo*," the man says. He turns his eyes skyward and crosses himself. "Why, Father? Why do you put this burden on me?"

"Why don't you get rid of her then?" Jack asks him.

The old man spits. "I want nothing more." He shakes his head miserably. "But I cannot. She is my curse."

"She looks like a donkey to me."

"It is only to fool you. Ha!" He makes a sign with his fingers and shakes them at the donkey. "She is no donkey. It is to trick you."

"If she's not a donkey, what is she?"

"She is my wife."

"I don't understand," Jack says. "Your wife?"

The old man nods vigorously. "She die five years ago." He leans close. "She was a powerful *bruja*, a witch, you know? She hates me her whole life, says it is my fault for everything bad that happens. When she die, she curses me. She say she comes back to torment me. Bah!"

Jack looks at me, one eyebrow raised. I shrug. He looks back at the old man.

"What makes you think the donkey is your wife?"

"Because they are the same. Both stubborn. Both like to bite."

"That sounds like most donkeys," Jack says.

The old man points at his eyes. "In her eyes. I see it there. She is looking out at me, laughing. Always laughing."

He picks up a rock and throws it at the donkey. The rock bounces off the donkey's side. She ignores it. The whole time she is staring at the old man. She has been since we stopped. I have to admit it's a little eerie.

The old man looks from one of us to the other. He has an angry look on his face, like he's waiting for us to tell him he's crazy. Jack nods and looks thoughtful. I'm not willing to go so far as to say the donkey really is the old man's dead wife, but I'm not saying there's no chance either. I've heard stranger things. Seen some too.

We got the fire going and cook up some of the beans we brought with us. The old man rummages around in his sack and comes out with a clay bottle. He opens it, takes a drink and hands it to my father. Jack takes a drink and right away his eyes start watering.

"That there's bumblebee whiskey, sure enough," he gasps, handing it to me. "Got a sting to it." He shudders and looks a little green.

I make sure I only take a sip. It's even worse than I expected, and I have to fight to not spit it on the ground.

The old man cackles. "Is not for children. You must be strong to drink my whiskey." He bangs on his chest. That sets off a coughing attack that seems like it will go on forever. It doesn't stop until he takes another drink of the homemade hooch.

With a bit of liquor in him, the old man gets downright friendly. He tells us about the village he lives in way up in the mountains. Says he's got six children still living, eighteen grandchildren and too many great-grandchildren to bother counting. He whispers to us that some of those offspring didn't come from his wife. Says he was quite the ladies' man in his youth and he's still got plenty of pep left. He leers at us.

Finally, he gets around to asking about us.

"Why come to the mountains?"

I figure Jack will tell him some story. I'm surprised when he says, "We're looking for treasure."

The old man stops with the corn whiskey halfway to his mouth. A smile twitches his lips. "The Heart of the Empire?"

"You know of it?" Jack asks.

"Everyone knows of it. It is a legend. When the Spaniards came, Atahualpa know he must hide it. Machu Picchu is where he put it."

I'm giving Jack a look, trying to get him to shut up, but he ignores me. He digs around inside his coat and brings out the map. "We have a map."

The old man looks interested. "Can I see?"

Jack spreads it out for him. The old man puts some more wood on the fire for light and peers at it.

"We're stuck," Jack says. "We need the other piece of the map to tell us where in the ruins it is."

The old man studies the map silently. He points at the drawing of the owl. "*El tecolote*. I know this."

We both stare at him in surprise. "Is it at Machu Picchu?" Jack asks.

The old man shakes his head. "No. In the church."

Jack and I share a look. Jack wipes his mouth. "Where is this church?"

"In the valley. Not far from my village." He gets to his feet unsteadily and wobbles off into the darkness.

"How do you like that?" Jack says to me in a low voice.

"I can't believe it."

He grins. "I told you. Sometimes you have to let Lady Luck do her thing."

"I don't trust him."

He frowns at me. "What happened to you to make you so untrusting of your fellow man?"

"Let's see, I've been falsely accused of murders I didn't commit twice. One time they were going to hang me. The other time they put me in the Yuma Prison. I was left to die in an Aztec temple. And, oh yeah, my father lied to me to get me to come to Peru where I nearly got shot by a thousand soldiers."

"You're exaggerating. It was a few hundred soldiers at most."

"That's not the point."

"I can see you're still upset. We'll talk about it later when you're calmer."

"People often want to shoot you, don't they?"

He scratches his goatee. "It does come up more often than I'd like."

"You ever wonder about that?"

"People shoot at you a lot too. You ever wonder about that?"

"Don't try to turn this around," I say. "This isn't about me."

"Maybe it's time it was."

"Look, I'm not the one who..." I taper off as I realize he isn't listening anymore. He's looking past me. I turn, already knowing what I'm going to see.

It's the old man. He's standing there holding a black powder pistol that was old when Columbus first sailed to the New World. Probably it doesn't work, but the hole in the end of the muzzle looks awful big. A ball that size would do fearful things to a body.

So much for not being shot at.

"Now hold on, partner," Jack says calmly. "There's no need for that."

"I am tired of the donkey. Give me the horse," he says. The muzzle is moving around a lot. Between drink and age, I'd say his arms are getting tired fast.

"You're not taking Coyote," I say.

The old man laughs. "That horse is uglier than my donkey. The other one."

"Watch what you say about my horse."

"You should eat that horse."

"Now you're going too far," I say.

"You're not taking my horse either," Jack says.

"No more talk. Give me the horse." He waves the gun to show us he means business.

When he does, the ball rolls out the end and falls on the ground.

We all look at it. "Well, that's a pile of shit," the old man grumbles. "So much for that." He throws the pistol down. There's a boom and a tongue of flame as the pistol goes off.

The old man stands there, looking at us, his eyes wary. He's wondering what we're going to do now. "You can steal my donkey if you want," he says.

"Nobody's stealing your donkey," Jack says. "Come sit down by the fire and we'll have a friendly drink."

"You gonna shoot me?"

"Never crossed my mind. Come on. Sit down."

The old man sits down, picks up his clay jug and takes a long drink. He doesn't offer any around. Was he sharing before because he was hoping we'd get drunk and it would be easier to steal a horse?

"What are we going to do when it's time to go to sleep?" I ask Jack in English. "Is one of us going to have to watch him all night? Or are we going to tie him up?"

"Neither," Jack says. "He won't try again."

"You can't be sure of that."

"I am. I read men for a living, Ace. The cards are only half the game."

"You didn't read him too well when you let him get the drop on us."

"He got the drop on you. I was expecting it all along."

"And that part about getting a giant hole blown in one of us? How did you plan for that?"

"He wasn't going to shoot us. Look at him. He's as harmless as a kitten."

I look over at the old man. He's slumped over, barely sitting upright still. His head's lying on his chest. Right then he starts snoring.

"Come on. Help me get him in his blanket."

Chapter 22

The old man is still snoring away when we saddle up the next morning. Jack lays a coin on his chest.

"He did try to rob us," I say. "You remember that, don't you?"

"I remember him giving us the clue we need to find the treasure. I'd give him more, but that's all I have left."

I can't argue with that. "You think we can find that church he was talking about?"

"Easy as bees in a pie," Jack says.

That stops me. "Easy as what?"

"Bees in a pie."

"I never heard that one before. Why would bees in a pie be easy?"

"You're overthinking this, Ace. It's just something people say."

"I never heard anyone say it before you did."

"I'm better read than most is all."

"You don't expect me to believe that, do you? I bet you never read a book in your life."

"There's things to read besides books. Come on. Let's go. I can hear that treasure calling me."

We mount up and ride out. The donkey follows us for a way. Mostly she follows Coyote. She seems to have taken a shine to him. Coyote's having none of it. He tries to kick her a couple of times, but she dodges him without too much trouble.

"He's going to think we stole his donkey," I say.

"We're doing him a favor. What good is a donkey that won't carry anything?"

"For all that, I think he's fond of the beast."

"And that crazy stuff about his dead wife being in the donkey?"

I think of the Apache Kid turning into a raven and flying away. "Anything is possible."

It turns out finding the church isn't all that hard. There's only the one road and when we see a narrow, overgrown track leading off it that afternoon, we follow it. The church is at the end of it.

The church is tucked away in a little hollow between two peaks. Just down the slope from it is the jumbled remains of a village, vines and thick plants fast reclaiming it.

The church is surprisingly large, considering how far away it is from anything and everything. It's one of those built by the Spanish priests with thick, adobe walls, a tower with a bell in it, and a wide doorway with a thick wooden door. Crouched out back of the church, like a dying dog, is a little stone hut with a thatch roof. Smoke is coming out of the makeshift chimney.

"There's still somebody using this anyhow," Jack says.

We ride up to the doors and get down. I follow Jack up the steps. There's a big, heavy iron ring set in the door. He takes hold of it and pulls. With a creak, it starts to open.

Someone speaks from behind us.

"Hold it right there."

Chapter 23

I spin around, my hand going to my gun. There's an older man standing behind us holding a pick, a suspicious look in his cold, blue eyes. His beard is white. It's one of those beards that just a fringe all along his jaw, no hair on his cheeks or under his nose. It's trimmed very close and neat.

"What are you doing here?" He's speaking English. He's definitely not a Peruvian. He sounds like this fellow I met who said he was from some place called New England, wherever that is.

"We...we heard about your church and we wanted to see it," Jack says, careful to keep his hands out in the open. The man looks like he'd have no problem going after us with that pick.

That seems to be the right thing to say, because the man relaxes some. He still doesn't lower the pick, though.

"We met this old man and he told us of this beautiful church," Jack says, warming up to his story. "He said we had to come see it."

The man finally lowers the pick. He's wearing a homespun cotton shirt and a hat that looks like it's woven out of dried fronds. The trees those fronds come from grow thick around here.

"He did, did he?" he says. "One of the natives?"

"Yessir."

"The natives don't come around here much anymore. They have shunned this church." He sure doesn't sound happy about it.

"It's a very nice church," I say. I'm not sure why I say it. He gives me a sharp look like he thinks I'm making fun of him. I'm not. I make it a point not to make fun of people carrying heavy, pointed tools.

"When I first got here, thirty years ago, they came to church all right. But then that happened." He gestures at the ruins down the hill.

"What happened?" Jack asks.

"They had a shrine in the middle of their village, a horrible, pagan thing. I told them to remove it. They didn't want to. They said the old priest didn't trouble them about it." His lip curls when he mentions the old priest. There's bad blood there.

He hefts the pick. "So I went down one night and took care of it myself. Smashed it into a thousand pieces."

"And that made them abandon their village?" Jack asks.

"No, they abandoned their village after most of them died of fever. They said the fever was a curse, that the shrine was the only thing keeping them safe. The fools believed that once I destroyed the shrine, I let the sickness free. I told them the true sickness was in their hearts, that the fever was a punishment from God for worshipping false idols." He still sounds angry about it after all these years. "I told them their only hope was to repent, to renounce not just their heathen ways, but the lies of the corrupt Catholic church as well."

"I take it they weren't in the renouncing mood," Jack says.

"No, they were not. One day they picked up and left. They never came back."

He glares at us like somehow this is our fault. Jack and I exchange looks. I'm not sure what to say. Mostly I want to get out of here before he gets all stabby with that pick.

"Their loss," Jack says.

"Their *eternal* loss," he says. He gives me a sharp look when he says this. I've got no idea what it means.

"Can we go in?" Jack asks. "We came a long way to see this church."

The man considers this for a moment, then nods.

"I'm Jack, by the way. This here is Ace," Jack says.

"I am Elias, late of New Hampshire, the pastor of this church."

"We're pleased to meet you, Elias," Jack says.

Speak for yourself, I'm thinking. There's a smell of crazy around this man that's got me nervous.

Elias steps past us and pulls the heavy door open. He enters and we follow. He pauses in the vestibule to take up a candle. He strikes a match and lights it.

We pass into the main room. It's cold in here. Weak light comes in through small, stained-glass windows set high in the walls. The pews are made of thick, dark wood. Heavy dust lies everywhere. Our footsteps sound oddly muted.

We follow him down the center aisle. I glimpse statues set into niches in the walls, old men with long beards and sad faces. We come to the altar. It is ornately carved and edged in gold trim. Behind it looms a large crucifix, twice the height of a man. The face is shrouded in shadows. The whole place is creepy. I keep expecting something to charge at us out of the shadows.

"It is a relic of the papists and I should have destroyed it long ago," Elias says. He's looking at the crucifix. "But somehow I never had the heart." His voice echoes around the room. I look over my shoulder.

"It's quite a church," Jack says. Elias is turned away and Jack points at the floor off to one side. Carved into one of the floor tiles is an owl. It looks just like the one on the map. He grins at me. "Those old Spaniards knew how to build. This place must be what, three hundred years old?"

"Easily." Elias turns back to us.

"What brings a preacher from New Hampshire all the way down to a Catholic church in the Andes Mountains?" Jack asks.

"God told me to come here. I did not question Him. I found a flock in need of a shepherd. The old priest had died only weeks before."

"And they never came back?" Jack asks. "Even after all these years?"

"Never," Elias says bitterly.

"If you don't mind my asking, why'd you stay? What with having no flock at all? Why not go somewhere else?"

Elias looks like he does mind Jack's asking. "God sent me here for a purpose. I will not deny Him." His jaw sticks out angrily. He looks like he wants Jack to challenge him.

But Jack surprises me by saying, "Spoken like a true man of the cloth. Such men as you are difficult to find in these fallen times."

That settles Elias' feathers all right. The hard look softens, and he almost smiles. "Truly your words are a balm on my soul. It is good to find a man of true faith."

I almost choke on my tongue when he says this. The only church my father ever sets foot in is a saloon. His god is a deck of cards.

But Jack lowers his head humbly. "Thank you, Elias. I know I am a terrible sinner, but the Lord knows I try my best. I only hope it is enough."

I want to laugh and cover it with a cough. Elias ignores me. He's all fixed on Jack right now.

"So long as you judge yourself harshly, it may be that you will find His mercy. This is a blessed day, indeed. I want to extend an invitation to you to stay the night here in my home and partake of my bread." He's staring at Jack while he says this. I get the feeling his invite doesn't really include me.

"Why, we'd be much obliged," Jack says.

"I will go straightaway and add more venison to the pot," Elias says. "There is a small shed where you may put your saddles." He motions for us to leave the church.

"Thank you kindly, Elias," Jack says. "If you don't mind, I'd like to stay behind for a minute. My heart aches with a need for some quiet prayer and it won't do the young'un any harm either."

Elias looks like he's going to argue, but then he nods. "I will see you inside."

"Why did you tell him that?" I ask, once he's gone. "I don't want to spend the night with him. He's ten pounds of crazy in a five-pound bag. We should make our own camp and sneak back in here after he's asleep."

"Why not take him up on the food? I'm tired of eating beans, aren't you?"

"Because he's crazy. Weren't you listening?"

"There's all kinds of crazy. He's the harmless kind."

"Says you. Also, I don't feel right about it. We're going to take his food and sleep under his roof and then rob him. It's bad medicine, is what it is."

"Rob him? Why do you have to say it like that?"

"Because that's what it is?"

"Is it robbing to take something a man doesn't even know he has? It's not his church anyway. It belongs to the Catholics."

"Yeah, it's still robbing. What would you call it?"

"I call it doing the Lord's work."

"What? Do you even know what that means?"

"Look at it this way. The Colonel is after us. That means sooner or later he's going to show up here. We don't know how much he knows. Maybe he came across the old man too. If he does, then he'll know about the owl and that there's something important behind it. He'll tear the whole church down if he has to. Probably shoot Elias while he's at it. Then, once he has the treasure, he's going to use the money to start a war where hundreds or thousands of people will die. Most of them poor peasants.

"Whereas, if we get the treasure, we're going to *help* people. Remember the well that went dry? Also, with the treasure I can pay off El Chacal, and not get eaten by his fish. That's another benefit. Everybody wins."

"You have an answer for everything, don't you?"

"I try."

I sigh. This is wrong in so many ways. But I know arguing with him isn't going to do any good. He's got his mind made up, and there's no changing it. "All right. We'll stay."

Jack's not listening. He's crouching by the tile with the owl on it. It's half under the first pew. "We should be able to take these tiles up with that pick he was carrying, no problem," he says.

Oh, boy. This keeps getting better and better. I sure hope the white man's hell isn't real, because this seems like the way to get there.

Chapter 24

"There's my lost sheep," Elias says when we come inside. "I was starting to think the talk of the curse ran you off." He's looking at me when he says this.

"I've spent the last few days around him," I say, pointing at my father. "I'm already cursed. What's one more?"

"Very funny," Jack says.

"I thought so."

We sit down at the table and the preacher serves us up some of the venison stew. I'll admit, it smells powerfully good. I didn't realize how hungry I was. I pull my bowl over closer and jam my fork in.

Quick as a wink the preacher cracks me on the back of my hand with the serving spoon.

I drop the fork and jerk my hand back. "Ow. What was that for?"

"This is the house of the Lord. You don't eat His food without a prayer first."

"You could tell me instead of whacking me."

"I've found that a dose of pain makes the lesson take better."

"You know how to swing a spoon," Jack says. "Brings to mind my dear departed mother. She could swing a frying pan with a vengeance."

"I'm sure she was a saintly woman," Elias says. "Let us bow our heads."

We bow our heads and he starts in. I figure out pretty quick that this isn't a prayer at all. It's a full-blown sermon. I've only sat through a couple in my life, enough to know I don't cotton to them. Now it looks like I've got to sit through one more.

Elias goes on and on, talking about heathens that won't turn away from false gods, about the lake of fire that's waiting for them. As one of those heathens he's talking about, I have to admit that such talk makes me uneasy. A lake of fire? Forever? I had no idea the white man's god was so angry. I'm liking the idea of stealing from the church less and less. If tangling with Totec taught me anything, it's that gods are best left alone.

Meanwhile, my stew is getting cold. I can see the fat starting to clump up on top. I'm tempted to make a go for it anyway, but I notice that Elias never sets down the serving spoon. He's waving it around while he talks, jabbing like it's a sword, swinging it like a club. I don't fancy catching it upside my head.

I glance over at Jack. He looks as miserable as I feel. That makes me feel a little better. At least I'm not the only one suffering. It was his idea to eat the man's grub anyway.

Elias wraps up his sermon with a good dose of fire and brimstone so hot I'm sweating under my coat. He stands there when he's done, looking from one of us to the other. He's waiting for something. I can see that much. Thing is, I don't know what it is. I look at Jack, but he looks perplexed too.

"Do either of you gentlemen have anything you want to say?" the preacher says. He says 'either', but he's looking at me.

I remember one of the cowboys on the Bar T ranch who liked to say, "Praise the Lord and pass the potatoes" but I'm thinking that wouldn't help here. Instead I say, "Amen?"

"Amen?" he repeats. He doesn't look happy with that. I don't understand why. I thought amen worked for everything.

"Amen, brother?" I say.

He's still not happy. "Is that all you have to say?"

I look to Jack for help, but he's not giving any. He's got a big grin on. I don't understand why the preacher is picking on me and not him. Next to Jack I'm practically a saint.

I've got one more thing to try and then I'm out of ideas.

"Praise the Lord," I say.

Elias scowls and shakes his head. The look on his face says he's found a real dumb one and he's asking the Lord for patience.

"I noticed your hair," he says.

It's hard not to, being down past my shoulders and all, but I don't bother to point that out to him. I have a feeling it won't help.

"You're an Indian, aren't you?"

I sit up straight and throw my shoulders back. "Apache." Yeah, I'm proud of it.

"Half," Jack says. The preacher ignores him.

The preacher points one long finger at me. "You are a heathen."

I've been called one before, but I'm still not sure what a heathen is. "Um…maybe?"

"Your people worship ravens and coyotes and such," he says. Which isn't right at all. We don't worship animals. That'd be foolish. But I can see he's riding this train to the end of the tracks. All I can do is go along for the ride. I hope the bridge isn't out.

"That makes you a heathen."

"I try not to be," I say.

"Trying is not enough." He swells up. It puts me in mind of a bullfrog when he's all puffed up looking for a mate. "You must cast the devil from your heart and ask the Lord to come in."

I don't think the devil is in my heart. Probably he has other things to do. But I want to get through this and eat my stew before it goes off. "I'll do it."

He smiles. "There. That wasn't so hard, was it?"

It wasn't so easy, either.

"I'll get my Bible," he says, and starts to turn away.

"Hold on," Jack says. "Aren't we going to eat?"

Elias turns back. "Eat?" He says the word like he never heard it before. "We can eat once I've baptized the heathen."

"Right now?" I say. My voice comes out kind of skittish. Because I am. I'm not completely sure what a baptism is, but I don't like the look on Elias' face.

"It's for your own good," Jack says, grinning even bigger.

"Exactly!" Elias thunders.

"Couldn't it wait until morning?" I say. I stand up. If this keeps on, I'm running. I'm not getting baptized until I know for sure what it is.

"Only the fool waits," Elias says.

"Ace has a point," Jack says. I know he's not doing this to help me. He doesn't want his stew to get any colder. "Morning would be better. New day, new start and all that."

"Hmm." Elias thinks about it. "I suppose you have a point." He looks at me. "You could spend the night in prayer then, preparing yourself."

"That's exactly what I mean to do," I say, nodding the whole time. No way I'm going through with this. If Jack wants that other half of the map so bad, let him get baptized for it.

"At the crack of dawn," the preacher says.

"At the crack of dawn," I repeat. I'm going to be so far away from here when that sun comes up.

Elias nods and sits back down. He picks up his fork. Jack and I dig right in.

The stew is good. Elias is wound a little tight, but he knows his way around a cookpot.

When the food is gone, Elias says, "That felt good."

"What did?" Jack asks.

"Preaching. It's been too long."

"I have to give it to you," Jack says. "Thirty years you've been waiting. I'd have given up a long time ago."

"It's a test of my faith. My devotion will be rewarded in time. Once the natives settle down, they'll realize how much they need the church."

I'm thinking that once they settled down, they realized how much they *didn't* need his church, but I keep that to myself. I ate the man's food, after all.

And I'm planning on robbing him later. That still eats at me.

I look at Jack, to see if this is bothering him too. But he looks like he doesn't have a care in the world.

"When that times comes," Elias says, "they'll find their church waiting for them. I'll be here to guide them back to the light."

I think he's going to be waiting for a long, long time. They already thought he was crazy before they started thinking he was cursed. Crazy and cursed isn't a good combination.

Chapter 25

Elias spends some time telling me all about my sins and then goes to bed.

We lay out our bedrolls and lie down on them. "We wait until he starts snoring, then we sneak out of here," Jack says. "Unless you want to stay for your baptism. I'm sure we could delay for a day if it's that important to you."

He laughs. If anyone needs baptizing, it's him.

It isn't too long before we hear snoring through the doorway. We gather up our gear, head out and saddle up. We might have to make a fast getaway. It's best to be prepared.

The pick is leaning up against the side of the house along with a shovel. We take them both and sneak into the old church. Jack lights a candle and we head on up to the front.

"This is a terrible idea," I say.

"You worry too much."

"We ate his food. We sat in his home. And now we're stealing from him."

"It ain't stealing if he doesn't know he has it."

"You said that already."

"It's still true."

"And what about breaking up the floor?"

"We'll be careful," Jack says, swinging the pick. On the first blow, the tile with the owl on it shatters into a hundred pieces. "Oops."

He takes another swing, shattering another tile. "You need to look at the big picture. We're staving off a war. That makes us heroes."

"Only you could turn robbing a church into something heroic."

"It's called perspective, Ace."

"I can think of other words for it."

"Are you going to help or only talk?"

In a few minutes he's got all the tiles destroyed in a good-sized area. I take the shovel and start digging. The ground is rock hard, and the going is hard. Then I hit something that sounds different. I tap it again. It's definitely not a rock.

"Give me that," Jack says, climbing down into the hole and taking the shovel from me. His eyes are all lit up like a kid with a sack of penny candy. He gets the shovel under a corner of it and pries it up.

It's an old, metal box about the size of a man's foot. He looks at me.

"You ready for this?"

"Stop wasting time. Open it up and let's get out of here." I look over at the door of the church, worried I'm going to see Elias standing there.

Jack has to hit the box with the shovel a couple of times, but he manages to get it open. Inside is something wrapped in cloth. He takes it out and unwraps something peculiar.

It's a piece of white stone about as long as my hand and about two fingers wide. One end is carved weirdly.

"What is this?" Jack wonders.

I look in the metal box and see there's a piece of paper in there still. I take it out. The paper looks the same as the half map we have. "Look at this."

Jack takes it from me, pulls the half map out of his pocket and holds the pieces together. They match perfectly. He looks at me, his eyes very bright. "This is it, Ace. The other half of the map."

I take a look. All that's on it is a drawing of an oddly-carved object. I can't tell what the object is or where it's supposed to be.

"How does this help?"

"I don't know. Hopefully it will make sense when we get there." He looks at the white stone. "Not sure what this is, but it must be important." He puts the map and the stone in his pocket.

Right then movement in the shadows behind Jack catches my eye and I look up.

It's Elias.

"I heard a noise," he says. "What are you two doing...?"

He sees the hole in the floor, the broken tiles scattered around. He lets out this horrified shriek that sounds like someone stepped on a cat.

"What have you done?" he screams.

And that's when I notice something else, something he's carrying that I didn't see at first.

A double-barreled shotgun.

Chapter 26

"I'll kill you!" he screams. "I'll kill you both!"

Jack's fighting to get out of the hole. I'm reaching for my guns, but I hung my gun belt on the back of a nearby pew when I started digging.

The shotgun barrel comes around, the holes in the end bigger than any holes I've ever seen before, bigger than my whole life...

There's nothing we can do. No chance either of us can move fast enough. It seems like I can already feel the buckshot ripping through my flesh.

Elias squeezes the first trigger.

Click.

For a half second we all stare at each other, every one of us surprised. Elias looks down at the gun in disbelief.

I don't know why his gun didn't fire, but I'm not wasting time thinking about it. There's a saying about not looking a gift horse in the mouth and I'm following it. Survive first, wonder later.

"Huh. Forgot to reload that barrel," he says. "But I got another barrel."

The shotgun swivels my way. He raises it to his shoulder. I dive behind the pew right as the gun goes off. There's an awful explosion, a burst of flame that lights up the whole church for an instant.

The pew bucks, but it stops the blast.

I snatch my guns from their holsters. I can hear Elias reloading. I poke my head up. Jack is out of the hole, crouched behind one of the other pews, holding his pistol. Elias is up by the altar. How did he get in here without me hearing him? I wonder. Must be another door in the back of the church.

I could shoot him now and end this, but it doesn't seem right. If I brought someone into my home and he tore up my church, I'd be wanting to shoot him too. I can't hold that against the man.

"Let's be reasonable about this," Jack calls out.

"I'll show you reasonable," Elias spits, closing the shotgun. "See what you think."

Jack hits the floor as Elias cuts loose in his direction. Wood chips fly everywhere, and smoke drifts up toward the ceiling.

Elias swivels toward me. "I see you there, heathen!" he yells. "I was going to baptize you with holy water. Now I'm gonna baptize you with lead!"

I duck as the shotgun roars again. This time he tears a chunk out of the pew big enough to put your fist through. I can't imagine what that would do to me.

"I don't want to shoot you, Elias," Jack calls.

A glance shows me that Elias dropped the shells he was trying to load. He's down on his hands and knees chasing the cartridges around.

I'm done talking. It's time to scoot.

I jump up, cross the aisle, grab Jack by the scruff of his coat and start dragging him toward the front door. "We have to get out of here."

For once he doesn't argue with me. He grabs his hat and lights out for the door. I fire a couple of shots high to convince Elias to keep his head down and run after him.

We're almost to the front doors when I get an itch between my shoulder blades. I've been shot at enough to recognize the feeling. There's no time for thought, only action.

I tackle Jack. As we hit the floor, the shotgun goes off again. I feel a couple of pellets hit me in the butt, but mostly all it does is make a whole lot more wood chips. I do believe Elias is prepared to blow this church to pieces to get to us.

"Stop shooting, damn you!" Jack yells. "We're leaving already!"

While he's yelling, we're both moving, rolling to the sides to get behind the pews again. Another shotgun blast answers him.

This time we make it out the door before Elias manages to reload. Fortunately, the horses are still there, though Jack's mare looks about a whisker from bolting. She doesn't like all the explosions.

Coyote just looks angry. He probably is wondering what it is I do to make so many people shoot at me. I'm starting to wonder the same thing. I think it's the company I keep. I need to start being more particular.

We jump on the horses and gallop off into the darkness. We haven't reached the safety of the trees when Elias makes it out the door. "Betrayers!" he screams. "Devil spawn!"

The shotgun fires again, and again, but the range is too great now.

Chapter 27

We slow down after a few minutes. I shift in the saddle, feeling those pellets I picked up. They're not anything serious, but they're sure not comfortable.

Jack looks over at me. "Pick up some lead?" he asks.

"I did."

"You'll be all right."

"Is that all you have to say?"

"What else do you want me to say?"

"How about, sorry, I almost got you killed again."

"You're being dramatic. That shotgun was loaded with bird shot. You were never in any real danger."

"Even bird shot will kill you, if you get enough of it."

"It could." He sounds like he doesn't believe it though.

"Is there anybody you meet who doesn't take a shot at you sooner or later?" I ask.

"You haven't shot at me yet," he says, his tone joking.

"I've sure been wanting to."

"I run into my share of misunderstandings, it's true," he says.

"I think old Elias understood you fine."

"I've learned it's best not to let that sort of thing bog you down. It's best to put it behind you and face firmly toward the future."

"Spoken like a man who didn't pick up any buckshot recently."

"If it's that bad, we can stop, and I'll dig it out with my knife."

"It isn't that bad."

"Then you have nothing to complain about. We've got the other half of the map, and we know where the treasure is. I'd say the future is looking bright."

I have some things I'd like to say about his bright future, but I decide to let them be for now.

We ride for an hour, looking for a spot to stop and make camp. The mountains have gotten a lot steeper in the last day or so and there's nowhere to get off the road, so in the end we throw our bedrolls down in the road.

In the morning, I wake up to find someone pointing a gun at me. This is really getting old.

It's Myron. Standing over Jack is Lonnie.

"Don't even think about it," Myron says. "I threw your guns off into the bushes. There's nothing you can do."

Jack opens his eyes and sees Lonnie. He makes a face. "You're like a dead possum, the way you keep turning up," he says.

"You're not shaking us this time," Lonnie says. "This time we got you dead to rights."

Jack sits up. Lonnie takes a step back. He's holding his pistol with both hands. "Stay right where you are, or I'll shoot."

Jack yawns and waves him off. "You can leave off with the threats. The gun you're pointing at me says it all."

"Bet you're surprised to see us, ain't you?" Myron says. I can see he wants to turn and look at Jack, but he's afraid to take his eyes off me. "I bet you thought you were home free. But we're not as dumb as you think we are."

"I don't know if that's possible," Jack says.

Myron frowns, trying to figure out what Jack meant by that. He gives it up and starts talking again. "I knew we'd find you sooner or later. I told Lonnie you were going to skip town, that you'd be heading for Machu Picchu. I told him all we had to do was keep our eyes peeled and we'd come across you sooner or later."

"It's too early for all this talk," Jack says. "What do you boys want? Spit it out and let's be done with it."

"Want?" Myron says, his voice kind of high-pitched. "We want the map that we almost died stealing. The map you cheated us out of."

"Cheat is a harsh word," Jack says. "Are you sure that's the word you want to use?"

"Ain't no other word for it!" Lonnie bursts out. "What you done is cheated us, plain and simple."

"I prefer to think of it as changing the terms of our agreement," Jack says.

"That's what you call leaving us to get caught by the Colonel?" Myron says. "Changing the terms?"

"It's one way to put it."

"Another way to put it is that you left us to die," Lonnie says, his face getting dark.

"I didn't leave you to die. I knew you boys would be okay. You're resourceful, I've always said that. Why, look at how you followed me way up here into the mountains."

"Don't try buttering us up," Myron warns. "It won't work. Not this time. We got the guns. We call the shots."

Lonnie looks at me. "You know your partner here is a low-down skunk, right?" he says.

"He's not my partner," Jack says. "He's my son."

"Son?" Myron says. "But he's...he don't look like you. Are you sure?"

"I know," I say. "I'm surprised by it too. I keep hoping it's a mistake."

"Very funny," Jack says.

"I feel sorry for you," Lonnie says, "having a back-stabbin' weasel like this for your father."

"Skunk. Weasel. You ought to watch what you say, Lonnie," Jack says. "Putting a man down in front of his only son is a low thing to do."

"He's got a right to know," Lonnie says.

"What happened?" I ask.

"I already told you," Jack says. "They got greedy and—" But Lonnie waves his gun at him and he shuts up.

"I want to hear it from them," I say. I'm getting a strong feeling there's more than one story here.

Jack reaches into his coat and pulls out the envelope. "You want the map? Here it is. Take it."

Lonnie snatches it out of his hand. Keeping an eye on Jack the whole time, he tears it open and takes out the paper inside. I notice it's only half the map, the part Jack mailed me. Lonnie looks it over.

"I'll be damned. It *is* hidden in Machu Picchu."

"I told you," Myron says.

Lonnie stuffs the map inside his coat.

"You got what you wanted, now go," Jack says.

"Not till I tell your son the truth," Lonnie says.

Jack looks at me. "It's all lies."

"I ain't said nothing yet," Lonnie says.

111

"That doesn't change anything."

"The soldiers showed up. He told us to hold the front doors," Myron says. "Hold them off for a minute, he says. I'll get the map and be right back. I know a way we can get out of here."

"But he never came back," Lonnie snarls. "He ducked out a back window and left us to get caught."

"He never told us that was who we were robbing, neither," Myron says. "He didn't say it was Colonel Guzman. I'd have never agreed to it if I'd known it was him. I thought we were only stealing something from the government."

I look at Jack. I can see in his eyes that what they're saying is true.

"I can explain," he says. "There were extenuating circumstances."

"If by that he means he betrayed his partners, then that's true," Lonnie says.

Things are starting to click into place. "They were your partners?" I say to Jack. "You didn't hire them?"

"Partners," Myron says. "Even split three ways."

"And you left them behind to get caught by the law?" I ask, thinking of Boyce hitting me over the head and leaving me to get caught by the posse.

"It wasn't like that," he says.

"It was too!" Myron bursts out. "You straight up left us to the Colonel." He shivers as he says this.

"I repeat," Jack says, "extenuating circumstances."

"The hell you say," Lonnie says. "You planned to let us take the fall all along. I should shoot you right here." He raises his pistol.

"Now, now, let's not be hasty," Jack says.

"You see now what kind of man your pa is," Lonnie says.

"I already had a pretty good idea," I say.

"How'd he rope you into this anyway?" Lonnie asks.

"He sent me a telegram in San Francisco. Said they were going to kill him if I didn't bring the map."

"Oh, boy, that's a good one," Myron says. "Leastways, now you know better."

"Yeah," I say, staring at Jack the whole time. "Now I know better."

"I think we should shoot him," Lonnie says.

"You'd shoot an unarmed man?" Jack says, putting his hands up. "In front of his son?"

"That does seem kind of heartless," Myron says. "I don't know how I feel about that."

"I always said you have a soft head," Lonnie says to Myron. "Now I know it's true." He points his gun at Jack's foot. "Maybe I'll just shoot him in the leg."

"There's no call to shoot me at all," Jack says. "You got the map. You won. Isn't that enough?"

"It feels like it's missing something," Lonnie says.

"The Colonel's behind us," Myron says. "Why not tie him up and leave him for the Colonel? Do to him what he done to us?"

Lonnie nods. "I like the sound of that. It puts everything square."

"The Colonel's coming?" Jack asks. For the first time he looks worried.

"We saw him yesterday," Myron says.

"How far back?" Jack asks.

"Not far enough," Myron says. "We should get going, Lonnie. I feel like he's going to pop up any second." To me, he says, "That man frightens me. I don't want him getting his hands on me."

I know what he's saying. I only saw the man from a distance, but I could feel it too. He's not the kind of man you want to get crossways of.

"You're right," Lonnie says. "Grab that rope off my horse." He scowls at Jack. "I still feel like I ought to at least put one hole in him. He's caused us a powerful lot of trouble."

Myron hustles off for the rope. A few minutes later they've got us trussed up to a couple of trees.

"That'll hold them, don't you think?" Myron says, stepping back to admire his work.

"It doesn't have to hold that long," Lonnie says. "Just till the Colonel gets here."

"There's no call for this," Jack says. "At least let my son go. Your beef's with me, not him."

"Sorry," Myron says to me. "You understand we can't do that, right?"

"Teach you to be more careful who you run with," Lonnie says.

"It's his pa," Myron protests. "A man don't get to choose his pa."

That's for sure.

Lonnie tugs on a couple of the knots to make sure they're secure, then nods and holsters his gun. He grins at Jack.

"The wheel turns, Jack. Now it's your turn on the bottom. See how you like it."

"Not much, I'll admit," Jack says. "But like you said, the wheel turns. I expect I'll be back on top before too long."

"We'll see what the Colonel has to say about that," Lonnie grunts. "Could be your wheel's coming off and you're headed for a ditch."

"That doesn't really fit the metaphor," Jack says.

"Then how about a bullet hole?" Lonnie growls. "Does that fit your metaphor?"

"What's a metaphor?" Myron wants to know.

"It don't matter," Lonnie says. "Let's get out of here."

They mount up and in a minute it's just the two of us.

Chapter 28

"That didn't work out too bad," Jack says. "No one got shot anyway."

"You got lucky," I say. "If it was me in their shoes, I'd have shot you."

He stops working on his ropes and looks at me. "You seem upset."

"You think?"

"I understand if you're a little riled. Here we were so close to having our hands on that treasure and—"

"You really think that's what I'm mad about?"

"It's kind of a big thing."

"I'm mad at you because you lied to me. And I'm mad at me for being dumb enough to believe you. I should have known better."

"Now, Ace. We've been working so well together. You're not going to let those two come between us, are you?"

"It's not them coming between us, it's you." There it goes again, my voice getting high, like I'm some wet-behind-the-ears dumb kid. "You lied to me."

"You mean about them being my partners?"

"I mean about everything! You lied to get me into this. And since then you've done nothing but lie."

"I'm sorry. I should have told you they were my partners. I thought it would only complicate things."

"Shut up for a minute, will you, Jack? Just shut up. I'm mad about the lying, sure, but that's not the half of it. Hell, I know you're a liar. I didn't expect anything different."

"Those are harsh words, son."

"Don't call me son. I'm not your son and you're not my father. And shut up. I'm still talking. The lying I could handle, but finding out you betrayed your partners and left them to die, that goes too far."

"They were exaggerating—ouch!" He breaks off as I kick him in the leg. I wish I could kick him in the head, but he's too far away.

"Only the lowest kind of snake betrays his partner," I hiss. "Were you going to do the same to me? Toss me aside as soon as the Colonel closed in?"

His eyes get wide. "That's crazy. I'd never do that to you. You know that!"

"Do I? I'm starting to think I don't know anything about you. Oh wait, yes, I do. I know you're the kind of man to abandon his own son, not once, but twice. You abandoned my mother. And you abandoned your partners. I'm starting to see how it really is."

For the first time he gets rattled. "Damn it, Ace! We went over this already. I didn't abandon you and your ma. I just…I couldn't live my whole life there in the stronghold. I'd go crazy. I ain't cut out for that kind of life. Shoot, look at you and the wild times you've had. Clearly you can't take that life either, or you'd still be there. Aren't you like the chief there or something?"

That hits a little close to home, but I'm not letting him sidetrack me. I'm too angry.

"What was your plan once we got the treasure? How were you going to cut me out of it?"

"I wasn't going to cut you out, I swear."

"That's what you say. But we both know you'll say anything to get what you want. Sooner or later you were going to run off during the night. Don't deny it."

"It doesn't matter what I say, does it?"

"Not really."

While we're talking, I've been shifting around so I can get a hand in my boot. Now I manage it. I get my fingers on the hilt of the knife I keep there. I pull the knife out. Jack's eyes light up.

"You're something else, aren't you? You always have another card up your sleeve. I knew I could count on you. Well done."

I don't bother answering him. I'd as soon never talk to him again.

The blade is sharp, and I have the ropes cut in a minute. I stand up, rubbing my wrists.

"Now me," he says.

Looking at him the whole time, I deliberately put the knife back in my boot. He sags a little.

"Oh, come on…"

I walk over and fetch my gun belt. I appreciate those two not taking my guns and leaving me out here unarmed. They're not bad fellers, only a little riled. As they should be. I pick up my hat and knock the dust out of it.

"All right. You made your point. I'm sorry. Truly. I'll make it up to you, I swear."

"I'll be seeing you," I say and whistle for Coyote.

"You can't do this, Ace."

"Watch me."

"I'm your father."

"No, you're a no-account gambler that my mother took pity on. I don't have a father."

He's starting to get desperate. I can see the whites of his eyes. "What do you want from me? Tell me and I'll do it."

"Nothing. I want nothing at all from you."

I mount up and ride away without looking back. He calls my name a couple of times, but I can't hear it.

Chapter 29

I spend the next couple of hours trying not to listen to my thoughts. They're all kinds of confused. I feel mad. I feel sad. I feel guilty.

I feel confused.

Why should I feel guilty? Jack brought this on himself. He deserves whatever he gets.

Coyote is acting weird. He keeps stopping and trying to turn back.

"We're not going back," I say after the third time. "I'm done with him."

Coyote turns his head and gives me a look. I've seen that look before.

"You don't know anything," I tell him. "What do you know? You're only a horse. You don't understand people stuff."

Still with the look. The guilty feeling gets worse.

"You know if I stuck with him, he was only going to betray me like he does everyone? It's the truth."

He twitches his ears and swishes his tail. It means he's getting angry.

"Is it because I didn't untie him first? That's stupid. He'll get out of it. They're only ropes. He'll figure it out."

He lays his ears back.

"Yes, I know the Colonel is somewhere in these mountains. You don't have to remind me. But it's not my problem. He needs to finally own the things he's done."

I can see Coyote still isn't buying the poke I'm selling. I'm not sure I am either. Yeah, I'm mad at Jack, but leaving him tied up like that isn't right.

"Okay. You win," I say to Coyote. "We'll go back."

Coyote's head turns and his ears swivel forward. I hear it a second later, the sound of hooves on rock.

I start to turn and run for it, but right away I know that's a bad idea. I'm on a straight stretch of road. Those riders are too close. They'll see me for sure. There's only one thing I can do.

I rein Coyote off the road. It's not easy. The terrain is mighty steep and the trees and such are thick. We manage to get less than thirty feet off the road. It's not near far enough, but it'll have to do.

I work around to a spot where I can see the road.

Here they come. There looks to be about thirty of them. Right in the middle is the Colonel on his tall, black horse, smoking a long, thin cigar. He's wearing all black, black coat, black hat, black gloves. His wide-brimmed hat is pulled low. I can't see much of his face, but enough to see that his skin is unnaturally pale.

The soldiers ride like men who fear their leader, staying as far away from him as they can, keeping their faces turned away. They're like a pack of dogs with a lion in their midst.

All except one, anyway. He's a barrel-chested man on a shaggy, gray gelding. He's wearing the same green coat and white belt as the others, but he carries himself like a man used to giving orders. Probably a sergeant then. He sticks close to the Colonel.

No one notices me. The soldiers have their heads down. All they want to do is survive this and get out of the mountains. This is a long way from anything they're used to.

Then the Colonel's head turns my way. I tense, sure he is going to see me.

His head turns away, and I let out a sigh of relief. That was way too close.

I give them a few minutes and head back to the road. The last of the soldiers is disappearing around a bend in the road. We trot after them.

Now comes the hard part. Somehow, I have to get ahead of the soldiers. But I don't see how. Coyote and I could leave the road and try to circle around, but it's going to be slow going. We won't even be able to keep up with them, much less pass them.

Could I create a distraction that draws them back? Then hide off to the side and go by them?

It's a weak plan at best, but there's not much else that occurs to me.

119

"We're likely both going to get killed doing this," I tell Coyote. "I hope you're happy." Coyote ignores me. He always does that when he knows I'm right.

I fire some shots over their heads and let out a few war cries. The soldiers in the rear turn and return fire. I shoot back and get ready to run once they come after me.

But they don't. The Colonel shouts something I can't hear, and they continue their march.

What am I supposed to do now?

The answer is nothing. Hopefully, the Colonel won't shoot Jack straight away, and I'll get a chance to rescue him.

I follow them to the place where Jack and I were tied up. I wait for the shouts and the gunshots. But I don't hear either.

I edge closer. I can see a few of the soldiers. They've stopped. I can't see anything else, though, and I can't really get closer.

A couple minutes later they start moving again. I get up to the spot and see that Jack is gone. All that's left are the ropes.

"See? I told you he didn't need our help," I tell Coyote. It feels good to be right, even if Coyote will never admit it.

But when I pull on the reins to go back the way we came, Coyote won't budge. When I keep trying to turn him, he rears up.

"You're showing no more sense than a fox in a farmhouse," I tell him. "Whatever happens here on out isn't our problem."

Coyote sets out after the soldiers.

"What's your problem, Coyote? Jack got himself free. This is no business of ours."

I might as well be talking to a rock. Coyote pays me no mind. He just keeps clomping along, being as pig-headed as ever.

"Most people have normal horses," I tell him. "Horses that do what they're told. Why can't you be a normal horse?"

He turns his head and fixes me with a look. He's never heard such nonsense.

"When this is over, we need to have a talk," I tell him. "Only one of us can be in charge. It's time you learned that."

His answer is a little sidestep that catches me unaware. The sidestep runs me right into a tree limb overhanging the road. I come this close to getting knocked off.

"It's going to be like that, is it?" I say once I get settled right in the saddle again. I spit out a couple of leaves. "We'll see who springs for oats next time I stable you. You might not even get any hay."

Coyote swishes his tail and leaves it at that. He knows he won this round. I know it too.

I don't win very often.

Or ever.

Chapter 30

Around the end of the day I hear shouts up ahead, followed by shots. Without thinking, I draw my pistols and gallop ahead. In my mind I can already picture my father lying slumped in the road in a pool of his own blood. Why did I leave him?

I come tearing around a corner ready to blaze away, but what I see has me hauling hard on the reins instead.

It's Jack and his two former partners, standing there with their hands in the air. All the soldiers are pointing guns at them.

Lucky for me none of them are looking my way. I turn around and get back out of sight before I'm spotted. Quick like I drop down, pull my rifle from the boot, and make my way through the trees to where I can see.

I get into place in time to see Jack and the other two drop their guns. Soldiers move up and surround them. They're thumped a couple of times and dragged over to the Colonel, who climbs down off his horse and lights a fresh cigar.

"We meet face to face at last," Colonel says. He has a soft voice, low and dangerous sounding. "I've been wanting to meet the man who has caused me so much trouble."

Jack smiles. He's cool under pressure. I'll give him that. "I think what we have here is a case of mistaken identity. You have me confused with someone else, Colonel. I am simply an honest man making his way through the mountains with two friends."

"Yet when we arrived, it seemed the three of you were only seconds from shooting each other."

"A simple misunderstanding, I assure you."

"It's not a misunderstanding," Myron blurts out, ignoring Lonnie, who's trying to shush him. "He cheated us. We just came up here to get it back."

The Colonel turns his eyes to Myron, who shrinks. He's wishing now that he'd kept his mouth shut.

"What is it that you came to get back from him?"

Myron's eyes dart around, but he sees no escape. "Uh…nothing really. Forget I said anything."

"I insist on knowing."

"You idiot, Myron," Lonnie hisses. The Colonel jerks his chin and the barrel-chested sergeant punches Lonnie in the stomach, doubling him over.

The Colonel looks back at Myron. "I'm waiting."

"He…he took a map."

"And this was *your* map?"

"Not…not exactly."

The Colonel puffs on his cigar and lets smoke trail from his nostrils. "What does that mean? Is it your map, or isn't it?"

"Not really," he says in a small voice. "We sort of stole it."

"Who did you steal it from?" The Colonel's dark, intense eyes are fixed on Myron.

Myron looks like a mouse that wandered into a lion's den. He wants to run, but there's no way past the lion. "It was…we stole it from you."

"Indeed, you did."

"We didn't know it was you we was stealing from," Myron babbles. "Else we'd never have gone along with it."

Lonnie thinks he sees an opening and jumps right in. "We're the victims here too, Colonel. We didn't know it was yours." He pulls the map out of his coat and holds it out. "Look, we got it back for you and everything."

The Colonel nods and the sergeant takes the map from Lonnie, then punches him again.

"What was that for?" Lonnie gasps. "I gave you the map."

The sergeant ignores him and gives the map to the Colonel, who looks it over, then puts it in his pocket.

"So we can go?" Myron asks. It's about the most foolish question I've ever heard.

"Not a chance," the Colonel says.

"But we didn't know it was yours," Myron whines.

The Colonel nods again. This time the sergeant punches Myron. Myron collapses to the ground with a wheeze.

"Shut your damn yap, Myron," Lonnie says. Myron answers with a choking sound. Lonnie looks at the Colonel. "That polecat cheated us and left us to get caught. It ain't right. I hope I get to see you shoot him."

"Surely you knew his reputation before you joined up with him?" the Colonel says.

Lonnie hangs his head. "We did."

"Then you have only yourselves to blame. Do not blame the cat when it eats your canary. It is the cat's way to do such things. Blame yourself for letting the cat near the bird in the first place."

Lonnie frowns, not quite following along. "I still blame Jack," he says.

"It is a failing of a weak mind," the Colonel says. "As for me, I believe in knowing everything there is to know about my adversary before engaging him. Then I can use his own failings against him." He turns to Jack again. "Where is the other half?"

"I don't know," Jack says. "I don't have it."

"We met a preacher on the road who said you tore up a big hole in the floor of his church."

"What do you know? Probably the same preacher we met. The man is missing a few spokes in his wheel, if you know what I mean."

The Colonel holds out his hand. The sergeant walks over to Jack, who reaches into his coat and takes out the other half. The sergeant gives it to the Colonel.

"There was *another* piece?" Myron wails, still lying on the ground. "I told you we didn't have the whole thing, Lonnie." Lonnie goes to kick him, but Myron grabs his foot and bites down on his ankle.

"You bit me!" Lonnie hollers.

"You tried to kick me."

The Colonel turns a dark look on them and they both go still. The Colonel looks at Jack again.

"You have caused me a great deal of trouble, Jack." He smiles and holds up the second piece. "But in the end, something good comes of it."

"Well, then, everybody wins, right?" Jack says. "You got the rest of the map, which you wouldn't have without my help."

"That is one way to put it."

"Then I'll be going on my way."

That earns Jack a punch from the sergeant. I have to admit, I enjoy it a little bit. I've wanted to punch him a lot of times since I got here.

Bent over, Jack says to the sergeant, "Try using your words." The sergeant smiles broadly and slugs him again.

When he can stand up straight again, Jack says to the Colonel, "I'll take that as a no."

"I do have something to offer you," the Colonel says. "A wager."

Jack perks right up. The Colonel is speaking his language. "What do you have in mind?"

"A contest between the two of us."

Jack smiles. "I like the sound of this."

"I knew you would." The Colonel's smile looks like he borrowed it from a vulture. "You see, Jack, I know a great deal about you. I know you are an American. You have been in Peru for several years now. You have been involved in several shady deals, but always, when they fall apart, you manage to walk away untouched. There is a reason they call you Lucky Jack. Most importantly, I know you are a gambler. The type of gambler who would risk the last swallow of water in the desert on the throw of the dice. Tell me, is any of this incorrect?"

"That does sound a lot like me," Jack admits. "Tell me more."

"If you win, I will let you and your erstwhile partners go free."

"And if you win?"

"You die."

Jack nods. "Those are high stakes."

"What other kind of worth playing for? There is no thrill otherwise. You know this."

"What's the game?" Jack looks like he's trying to keep from rubbing his hands together.

"I think I will let that be a surprise." The Colonel pauses. "I will tell you this. It is a simple game. Perhaps the simplest game there is. At the end, there will be no doubt who the winner is." His smile gets wider.

"And who the loser is."

Chapter 31

The Colonel beckons the sergeant. "See to it that they do not escape."

The sergeant salutes. He barks an order and soldiers grab onto the three men. They are hauled over to a large tree. Manacles are placed on them. Then a chain is run through the manacles and around the tree and secured with a large padlock.

I fade back into the trees. What is the Colonel planning? I can't imagine the game will be fair. Surely the Colonel plans to cheat. There's no way he's going to let his prisoners go.

I need to figure out how I'm going to rescue Jack.

Over the next hour I come up with a dozen different plans and throw out every one of them. Jack and the other two are smack in the middle of the camp. There's no way I can see to get near them without being seen. The whole time the sergeant is sitting nearby, a rifle across his knees.

Maybe I could create a diversion and sneak into the camp then. I could try running their horses off.

But that's no good either. There are two men guarding the horses and they're staying on their toes. No one wants to screw up and have the Colonel mad at them. If I had all night, maybe someone would fall asleep and I'd have a chance, but I don't have all night. Whatever the Colonel has in mind, it's happening soon.

Finally, I have to accept that there is nothing I can do right now but wait. Maybe Jack will win the game, and the Colonel will keep his word. If he loses, maybe the Colonel will wait until morning to execute him, and I'll have a chance to rescue him during the night. They're slim maybes, even I can see that. But they're all I have. I bounce between cursing my father for getting himself into this mess and myself for leaving him tied up.

The soldiers build a fire and cook food. The Colonel spends his time writing in a tiny notebook. Figuring that this game, whatever it is, will happen by the fire, I make my way around the camp to a spot with a better view.

126

It's been dark for a while when the Colonel stands up and says, "It is time. Bring the prisoner."

The sergeant uncuffs Jack. Rubbing his wrists, he walks over to the Colonel. He has a glint in his eye. It looks like he's enjoying this. He really does love gambling more than anything.

"What's the game?" he asks.

"The game is Russian roulette."

The camp goes dead silent. Even Jack for once has nothing to say. He swallows. "Did I hear that right?"

The Colonel's smile is dark. "You did."

Jack rubs his goatee. "Wouldn't you rather play cards?"

"I have grown bored with cards. I have grown bored with most every game of chance. They are empty to me now. Taking a man's money is exciting, but taking his life...now that is something, don't you think?" His eyes glitter in the firelight.

Jack looks around for a way out, but there is none.

Jack takes a deep breath. "How many rounds?"

"Three."

"Only one cartridge in the gun?"

"Only one."

Again, Jack looks around. He's figuring his chances if he makes a break for it. They're bad. Much worse than the game offers.

"You're fixed on this game, then?" Jack says.

"Very much so."

He sighs. "Let's get it over with."

The Colonel holds up a hand. "Not so fast. I have not explained the rules to you yet."

"Not much to rules in this game, is there? I point the gun at my head and pull the trigger. I'm dead or I'm not."

"You may be surprised."

"If I do this, how do I know you'll let me live? How do I know you won't shoot me anyway?"

"You don't. You have only my word as a gambler."

"Gamblers lie all the time."

"True. Cheating is part of any game, perhaps the best part. I will cheat if I can, and you will cheat if you can. I expect nothing less. However, one thing I never cheat on, one thing I never lie about, is the stakes. I would never welsh on a bet. A gambler who does not pay up is no man at all, wouldn't you agree?"

Jack nods. "Still doesn't make me feel a lot better."

"Then console yourself with this. If you don't play, I will most certainly shoot you. A chance of not being shot, even a slim one, is better than no chance at all, wouldn't you agree?"

"When you put it that way."

"Are you ready to hear the rest of the rules of our game?" the Colonel asks. While he talks, he draws his pistol. He opens the cylinder and shakes out all the cartridges.

"I'm listening."

The Colonel returns one cartridge to the cylinder, snaps it shut and spins it. He looks at Jack and a peculiar smile crosses his face.

"I am playing too."

Jack's mouth all but drops open. "What? Really?"

"Really."

Jack frowns at him. "Why?"

"Why play any game of chance?"

"But this—"

"Answer the question, Jack. Why do you play games of chance? The truth now."

Jack doesn't have to think about this for long. "For the thrill."

The Colonel smiles. "Exactly. It is for this that I play as well."

"You're really going to hold the pistol to your head and pull the trigger?"

"I have never enjoyed watching games of chance. There are those who do. But they are fools. They will never know the thrill when the final card is turned, or when the dice come to a stop. They are but pale shadows, standing on the edges, trying to experience life through others, doomed to experience nothing."

Jack ponders this. "You're right," he says after a bit. He gives the Colonel a crooked smile. "You're *loco*, you know that?"

"Almost certainly," the Colonel says, spreading his arms wide. "I would not have it any other way. Shall we begin?"

"Are you going first?"

"No. You are my guest. I insist that you go first." He holds out the pistol.

Jack takes the gun. "And if we both go, and neither one dies?"

"Then we will continue the game. Understand this, there *will* be a loser in this game. I will not spin the cylinder again. Three rounds is the most this game will go."

Jack hefts the pistol. I know what he's thinking. Apparently, the Colonel does too, because he says, "Like any good gambler, you are weighing your odds. You are thinking about pointing the gun at me instead of yourself. Maybe you can shoot me and escape in the confusion. Is that it?"

"It has crossed my mind."

"As it should. A true gambler must weigh every option and choose the one that gives him the best odds. Let us go over them together. To begin, there is only a one-in-six chance that the chamber you drop the hammer on is loaded. Those are poor odds. Drawing to an inside straight almost. But, let's assume you get lucky and the chamber is loaded. I fall dead. What happens next?"

He gestures, and the sergeant points his pistol at Jack's chest.

"What are the odds he will miss you? Or that he will defy my orders?"

"Not good."

"Not at all. But let us be generous and say there is a one-in-twenty that one or the other happens and you emerge unscathed. At that point you will have to reckon with thirty other soldiers who will draw their weapons and try to shoot you. The odds that none will hit you are very poor, perhaps one-in-fifty. Stacked up against each other, those are terribly long odds, Jack.

"Now let us consider the other choice, the one in which you play the game. There your odds of being shot are only one-in-two. Surely, after examining both options, you see that there is only one choice to be made."

"It sure looks that way." Jack raises the pistol and points it at the Colonel. Soldiers reach for their guns, but the Colonel motions them to stand down. "How about you, Colonel?" Jack asks. "Are you willing to risk it?"

"Absolutely. But I already told you that."

Jack lowers the gun. "I wanted to make sure."

"No more stalling. It is time to begin."

Jack raises the gun.

I can't believe I'm watching this. Without realizing it, I've drawn both my pistols. I'm about a hair away from firing.

And then what? I can take out the sergeant, but after that? There's no way I'll get him out of there without both of us getting shot to doll rags.

I have no choice but to watch and hope.

"Can you feel it, Jack? Everything is brighter, sharper. Your nerves tingle, every one of them fully alive. It's the ultimate thrill. There is nothing else like it. In the next second you will live or die." The Colonel stares at Jack with burning eyes. His mouth is partway open.

Jack cocks the pistol and puts it to his temple. Amazingly, his hand is steady. He has nerves of steel. I feel sick. I want to look away, but I can't. I'm frozen in place.

Jack smiles and pulls the trigger...

Chapter 32

Click.

I exhale. I'm shaking badly.

"You survived!" the Colonel says. "Do you see what I mean now?"

Jack nods. "You're a crazy bastard, but yeah. I see it." He's grinning like he's the crazy one.

"Feel the blood in your veins. Feel the air in your lungs. You're alive, and nothing could be more thrilling. Only death can make life so precious." The Colonel looks ecstatic.

"You've played this before, haven't you?" Jack asks.

"Yes. But only one round. It is terribly difficult to find a partner for this game, and not nearly as fun alone."

Jack holds out the gun. "Your turn."

The Colonel takes it. He strokes it gently, like it is a holy object. "There is no other game like it." His eyes are partway closed. He's really enjoying this.

He's crazy as a bedbug.

He cocks the gun and puts it to his temple.

I look around. The soldiers are staring at him like someone dropped a rabid cougar in their midst. They knew their leader was *loco*, but they didn't know it was this bad.

It occurs to me that now might be the opportunity I've been looking for. But when I look closer, I realize that the sergeant isn't distracted like the others are. His eyes are still fixed on Jack, the gun in his hand steady. Even if I shoot him, he may still kill Jack.

The Colonel closes his eyes. He has a look of ecstasy on his face. He squeezes the trigger.

Click.

The Colonel stands there for a long moment without moving. He breathes deeply, his nostrils flaring. He opens his eyes.

"Exquisite. No wine could taste as sweet. No woman could match it. Truly, there is nothing else like it."

He hands the pistol back to Jack. "One-in-four now, Jack. The odds grow slimmer, the flavor sweeter."

"You really have a problem, you know that?" Jack says.

The Colonel shakes his head. "You disappoint me. I thought you, of all people, would understand. I have heard many stories about the crazy gringo from the north who would rather gamble than sleep or eat. I have watched you from afar. I know about your troubles with El Chacal. I know about the people who have tried to kill you because you were better at cheating than they were. And as I did, I said to myself, there is a man who understands living, who understands that a life without risk is no life at all."

"Maybe you don't know me as well as you think you do."

"It appears that this is true. Still, the game continues. Proceed."

Jack looks around the clearing. Every eye is fixed intently on him. People seem frozen. I feel it too.

"All right then." He says the words like he's talking to himself. He raises the pistol to his temple.

Click.

Jack breathes a huge sigh of relief. He's not the only one. I think everyone there does. Except the Colonel. He smiles.

"How is it this time?" he asks.

"You're right. There's nothing like it." Jack shivers.

"You see now."

"This is crazy, Colonel. I'll help you find the treasure. I know things you don't." He's thinking about the stone key. "We don't need to do this anymore."

"And miss this? I wouldn't dream of it. I have waited for this for too long."

"Like I said. You have a problem."

The Colonel's teeth are very white as he smiles. "Perhaps the next few moments will fix it."

He takes the pistol from Jack, cocks it, and holds it to his temple. He breathes deep. There is a peaceful look on his face that is disturbing, considering what is going on. He closes his eyes and squeezes the trigger.

Click.

The Colonel shudders. The look on his face…I can't describe it. I know I'm going to see it in my nightmares.

The Colonel hands the pistol back to Jack. "We are in the final stretch. Now we face the simplest, most elemental odds. One-in-two. One lives. One dies. There is no more delay."

Jack is looking at the pistol like he's holding a snake. "It comes down to this," he says.

"There was no other way it could end," the Colonel replies. "The true gambler realizes that, in the end, the only worthy wager is one's own life. Every other wager before was merely a prelude to this moment."

Jack cocks the pistol and puts it to his head.

I want to scream, but I can't find my voice. I have to do something, anything, but I can't seem to move. I see movement from the corner of my eye and realize that Coyote has moved up beside me. He is watching too, his ears perked forward.

Jack squeezes the trigger.

Crack!

Chapter 33

There's a sharp retort and a burst of flame. I flinch.

But something doesn't fit.

My father isn't lying on the ground in a pool of blood. He's still standing, holding the gun. He's looking at the gun in confusion. Everyone else is staring in disbelief as well.

Then I realize...

The gun misfired.

All of this happens in a heartbeat. My paralysis disappears. My hands know what to do even before I do.

I point with the right-hand gun and squeeze the trigger. The gun barks and a soldier staggers back, a red flower blooming on his chest.

The left is close behind, the two shots nearly indistinguishable. Another soldier goes down.

My next shot is meant for the Colonel, but he ducks behind a nearby soldier and the man takes the bullet I meant for him. The soldiers are starting to scatter now. I fire twice more into them and then leap onto Coyote's back.

Coyote knows what to do. He charges out into the mass of soldiers, scattering them with his hooves and shoulders. They are running like chickens fleeing the fox. The Colonel shouts an order, but they pay him no mind.

My father holds up his free hand—the other still clutches the pistol—and I grab it as we race on by. I swing him into the saddle behind me. Coyote barely slows down.

We gallop through the camp. Before us I see a soldier fighting to get his rifle up. Before I can shoot him, Coyote runs into him, sending him sprawling.

A few shots ring out behind us, but by that time we're on the road and the trees swallow us up.

Jack speaks for the first time.

"Took you long enough."

I twist to look back at him. It's mostly black under the trees, but we pass through an open patch and for a moment there's enough light to see his face. He's grinning madly.

"Is that all you have to say?"

"I was beginning to wonder if maybe you fell asleep."

"Did you forget the last time we spoke? Don't you remember me riding away cursing you?"

"I remember."

"Then how did you know I wasn't halfway back to Lima already?"

"Because I know you. I knew you wouldn't abandon your old man when he needed you." He wipes his forehead. "I have to admit, I was starting to worry. I kept thinking, okay, now would be a good time."

"What was I supposed to do?" I ask again. "I mean, what, exactly?"

"I don't know. Something fancy with those twin six guns of yours."

"Something fancy."

"I read the story. Twice. According to that newspaperman, you can shoot a gnat in the eye at a hundred paces."

"I can't shoot thirty men. Not before they fill you full of holes."

"You wouldn't have to shoot all of them. Only the ones causing problems."

"I should have left you with the Colonel. You two belong together."

"That guy. Is he crazy, or what?"

"Not any crazier than you."

"You're only saying that because you're mad. I don't get why you're mad. You're not the one who had to play Russian roulette."

"It's your own fault," I say. "You're unbelievable. You steal from the scariest man in the country. You betray your partners. You lie to get me to come help you. What's real, Jack? Tell me."

He squeezes my shoulder. "You are. I knew you'd come back for me. You're a good son."

I shouldn't care that he said that. I should push him off the back of the horse. I hate that I do care. Why should it matter at all what he thinks of me?

"You didn't stash another horse around here somewhere, did you?" he asks. "I'm tired of riding behind you."

"Of course, I have a horse for you. I have a coach actually. One with big, soft pillows like El Chacal's. It's right around the next bend."

"Give it up, Ace. You don't do sarcasm well."

Chapter 34

We ride through the darkness for hours. I can't hear the Colonel's men behind us, but I know they're there. I'd like to keep going, but I also know Coyote needs to rest. If we run him down now, we'll have no chance of running at all later. I wish I'd been able to steal one of their horses.

We try to get off the road, but there's nowhere to go. The mountainside is too steep, the forest too thick. We end up having to stop in the middle of the road. "We'll start again at first light," I say. For once Jack has nothing to say.

I sleep lightly, listening the whole time for anything out of the ordinary. It's hard, because in this forest, everything is out of the ordinary. Strange shrieks and howls split the night. More than once I sit up, gun in hand, as some gibbering noise dies away in the darkness.

"You worry too much," Jack says one time. I think I don't worry enough.

There's no way we can stay ahead of the Colonel without another horse. Even if we get to Machu Picchu before him, how are we going to get away? There's only the one road.

Who is my father, really?

In the first gray light of morning I get up and nudge Jack awake with the toe of my boot.

"Ow. Quit kicking me."

Okay, maybe it was more of a kick than a nudge. I'm still peeved.

"We have to go."

He sits up, rubbing his eyes. "I don't hear the soldiers."

"That's the point. We don't want to hear the soldiers."

He stands up and stretches. "How about I ride up front today, huh?"

"You must be out of your head. Why would I do that?"

"I don't want to complain, but—"

"But you're going to anyway."

"Think of it as constructive criticism. You're not making the best decisions when it comes to this escape plan of yours."

"There is no escape plan."

"Exactly."

I cross my arms. "What would you have done differently?"

"Well, I'd have a second horse. That one goes without saying."

"Right. Because just saving your life isn't enough."

"You need to think big picture, Ace."

"The picture I'm seeing is me leaving you here to walk and high-tailing it back to Lima."

"You'd never get past the Colonel and his men."

"There's gotta be other ways off these mountains."

"You sure about that?"

No, I'm not. The terrain was terribly rugged already, but during the night the road started to really climb, and it got a whole lot worse fast. The road itself is hard enough to follow. In most places it's barely a track. There's places where floods have washed out huge ruts like small canyons. Trees have fallen across it. Rocks have tumbled downhill onto it.

But off the road? It's a whole new level of terrible.

The mountainside is so steep a goat would have trouble on it. The trees and vines and ferns are thicker than ticks on a razorback. No wonder so many people carry machetes.

"This is your fault," I tell Coyote. "I told you we should have left him. We'd be safely in Lima by now."

"You're blaming your horse now?"

"Mostly I blame you."

He takes hold of Coyote's reins. "It's best if I ride up front. Trust me."

"Oh, that's never happening." I yank the reins out of his hand. "Besides, you try to climb on Coyote without me, he's liable to stomp you to death. You're lucky he lets you sit on his back at all."

"You're exaggerating," he says, scratching Coyote behind the ears. "He's nothing but a big pussycat."

For some reason Coyote not only lets Jack scratch him, he looks like he's enjoying it. That makes me even madder. Can't this horse see what I can see?

I push Jack's hand away. "Stop that. You're spoiling him." I swing up into the saddle, barely ahead of Coyote's latest attempt to bite me.

"What did you do to this poor horse to make him want to bite you all the time?" Jack asks, climbing up behind me.

"Shut up. You don't know anything."

We start riding again. The road gets even steeper. There's a spot that's so washed out we have to dismount so Coyote can jump across it. Even then, it's almost too far for him.

We haven't been going long when I hear the sound I've been dreading. It's a shout.

"They found our camp," Jack says. "It won't be long now."

I check the loads on my guns. Jack loads the pistol he took from the Colonel with rounds from my gun belt. I check the action on the Winchester. It's showing the first signs of rust, but it'll be okay. It's a durable rifle.

"We can't fight them off, and we can't outrun them," Jack says.

He's right on both points. Coyote is strong. He can run about any horse alive into the ground. But carrying two people is asking too much. I hear another shout. Closer now. I figure we have an hour at most before they catch up to us.

"You could stay behind," I say. "Hold them off so Coyote and I can escape."

"Give it up, Ace. Humor isn't your thing."

"I wasn't trying to be funny."

"Good. Because you're not."

"We could find someplace to get off the road and hide until they go by," I suggest.

"And let them get the treasure? Did you forget about the war already? You really want to be responsible for letting a man like that get into power?"

"How would it be my fault?"

"A good man cannot stand by while evil works its plans."

"What? Do you ever listen to yourself? Don't tell me you think you're the good man in this."

"I have my flaws, it's true. But I seek the higher good."

"Keep telling yourself that. You think the Colonel will want to play Russian roulette again, or will he straight up shoot us both?"

"I don't know. It's best if we don't fall into his hands again. I think he's a little crazy."

"He's a lot crazy. What were you thinking, stealing from him?" I ask.

"I might have misjudged him a little," Jack admits.

That surprises me. My father never admits mistakes. I'm going to take this as a win.

Not that it matters much. The Colonel is going to catch us soon. We won't get away again.

"What we need is a little luck," Jack says.

"You sure you didn't use all yours up last night?" I ask. It's something we haven't talked about yet. "How often does a cartridge misfire like that?"

"When a round gets old, or gets exposed to too much moisture—"

"Don't start. It's still no better than one in a hundred."

"Luck is a gambler's best friend. Surely I taught you that."

"You also told me luck is an evil hellcat."

"She is also that," he agrees. "I admit, when I pulled the trigger that last time, I thought my luck had run out for sure." He chuckles. "It's good to know she's still in my corner."

"You really think that, don't you?"

"Yes. I do. And now, I just need a little more."

"You're pushing it too far."

He pats me on the shoulder. "Have a little faith."

I hear another shout and look back. This time I can see them. They're still a few hundred yards back and quite a bit lower down, but they're closing in. We're running out of time.

"Well, would you look at that," Jack says.

I turn back to face the front. I can't believe what I see.

Chapter 35

"That's not...is that the old man?" I say.

"It is," Jack says. He sounds proud. Like he made it happen.

"That's impossible. The last time we saw him, he was way down the mountain."

"Luck comes through again."

I don't answer. What can I say? I hope the old man can help us.

We catch up to him. It's easy. He's still moving about as fast as a turtle with a broken leg, still tugging on the donkey's lead rope and cursing at her.

"Hello!" Jack greets him like he's an old friend, not someone who tried to rob us last time we saw him.

The old man looks up at us, blinking. "It's you. I wondered if you..." He makes a motion with his hand to indicate us falling down the mountain.

"Not yet," Jack says. He hops down, gives the donkey a pat on the back. "What brings you up here?"

Really? We're about to be gunned down by soldiers and my father is having a friendly chat?

"I go to my village."

I can't take this any longer. I swear I can hear hooves. "How did you get up here ahead of us?"

The old man's head swivels to me. He looks confused by my question. "I walk." He clearly thinks I'm touched to ask such a question. How else did he get here, fly?

"That isn't what I meant."

"What my impatient son means," Jack says, "is how did you get ahead of us? No offense, but you're not moving very fast."

"Ah," the old man says, his head bobbing. He taps his temple. "I know hidden ways."

"Hidden ways?" I blurt out. "There are hidden ways? Where?"

His eyes dart to me, then away. He shifts from one foot to the other. "Here and there."

I start to push harder, but my father cuts me off with a sharp look. "Forgive him. You know how the young are. What he's trying to say is that some soldiers are chasing us, and if we don't get off this road, they're going to shoot us."

The old man nods again. "That is no good, no good at all."

"That's one way to put it," I say. Jack glares at me.

"Can you help us?" Jack asks.

"Sí. Only, you must tell no one. Secret ways, no?"

"We promise," Jack says, but the old man is looking at me. "Ace, you have something you want to say?"

"I promise too," I say.

The old man is still looking at me. "You must walk. The trail is too small to ride."

I can live with that. I can live with anything that keeps me from getting shot. I climb down. "Where?"

The old man nods. He turns away and looks around. "Somewhere. Nearby, I think."

"You *think*?" I blurt out before I can stop myself. I can still mount up, I'm thinking. I can leave my father here with this crazy old coot. Coyote and I can stay ahead of the soldiers without him.

The old man frowns. Jack says, "Calm down, Ace. You're getting all lathered up."

"You know the soldiers will catch up to us in about a minute, don't you? And they're all carrying guns? Don't you think that's worth getting lathered up about?"

Jack shakes his head and turns away. "Don't mind him," he tells the old man.

The old man continues on up the road. I swear he's moving even slower than he usually does. He takes his machete out and pokes at the plants lining the road as he goes. I wonder if he's senile or if he wants us to get killed. Maybe that's his real plan. He means to delay us until the soldiers can finish us off. He still wants to get his hands on the map.

I glance back over my shoulder. Through a break in the greenery, I can see them. How did I get myself into this? What's wrong with me?

"I wonder what getting shot to death feels like," I say.

"Stop it, Ace," Jack says. "It's not that bad."

I don't even bother arguing with him. I draw my pistols. I'm not going down without a fight.

"Here it is," the old man says.

I look where he's stopped. He's wrong. There's no path there, only a wall of plants with wide, shiny leaves taller than I am.

He pushes some aside with his machete and leads the donkey in. The plants close and he's nowhere to be seen.

"Are you coming?" Jack asks, following after him.

Chapter 36

Calling what we're following a trail is like calling a dog a horse. They look a little like each other, but they aren't the same animal at all. For one thing, most of the time I can't even see the trail because the plants are so thick. If I wasn't right behind Jack, I'd lose it.

Once we're off the road a bit, the old man starts hacking with his machete, which helps some with the first problem. But it does nothing for the second one, which is that the trail is so narrow and steep that putting one foot down wrong will probably end up with me bouncing and rolling all the way back to Lima. The word cliff wouldn't be far off.

I look back at Coyote. "You got this? It's pretty steep."

In response he gives me a yellow look and shoves me with his nose. He's telling me I'm the one who should be worrying. He's doing fine.

After that I focus on watching my step. I wish I was wearing my moccasins instead of my boots. They're a lot better in bad footing. I'd get them out of my saddlebags, but I don't think I can get back to them.

After a bit I hear the soldiers behind us. It sounds like they got to the spot where we left the trail. I tense up a little. If they've got any halfway decent trackers with them, they'll figure out where we went easy enough and then we're in trouble.

But they go right on by without slowing down. I reckon they're not bothering to watch the tracks. Why should they? It doesn't look possible to leave the road. By the time one of them thinks to check, they'll have stomped all over our tracks and never find them.

And really, why bother chasing us anyway? They have the map. They don't have the key, but they don't know about it. Unless the Colonel is dead set on revenge, he's going to head right for the treasure.

The trees thin out a bit, enough that we get a view. It's something to see. The mountainsides are a deep, soft green like a thick blanket. There are steep canyons everywhere, with thin ribbons of rivers snaking down them. Knife-edge ridges and lofty peaks fill the horizon in every direction. If I didn't have to walk around in them, I'd think these mountains were right pretty.

The day passes and still we follow the old man on the path. Brightly-colored birds fly overhead. Swarms of butterflies appear and disappear as quickly. We pass waterfalls and trees with strange, twisted limbs.

It's getting down near the end of the day when he says simply, "We're here."

I look past him, thinking he must be joking. We're still on the side of a mountain. There can't be a village here.

But sure enough there is.

A whole section of mountainside has been terraced. It's like steps for giants. On some of the steps they're growing crops. I see corn, melons, squash and other things I don't recognize. Other steps have homes on them, simple huts made of wood with thatched roofs, half-dug into the mountainside.

A small stream splashes noisily through the village. Half-naked children run here and there, laughing and yelling. Women carry bundles in fiber nets. Two of the men are skinning an animal that's hanging from a wooden tripod.

A moment later everyone goes still and stares at us. It happens so fast it's eerie. No one calls out a warning, but in the space of a few heartbeats everyone notices and stops whatever they were doing.

"Hello!" Jack yells and waves.

That causes about half of the children to bolt for shelter. The others hide behind their parents.

"You're good with children," I say.

"They'll come around. A couple of card tricks and I'll have them eating out of my hand."

The worst part is, he's probably right. Everyone who doesn't know Jack loves him. It's once you get to know him that you realize your mistake.

The old man leads us into the village. They're shy at first, but it doesn't take long before they gather around. They must not ever get out of the mountains because they're amazed by just about everything. The boys and young men want to see my Colts. I take one pistol out and let them look at it, but I don't let anyone hold it. I don't want anybody shooting himself.

One old man who's wearing a feather head dress and a whole lot of strings of beads is taken with my duster. Probably he's their chief. He keeps stroking my coat. It's a little strange. I'm glad when he goes away.

The little kids can't stop staring at Coyote. They probably never saw a horse before. The village has a couple of donkeys, along with some goats and some kind of animal that looks like a goat with a long neck, but no other horses. It's not really horse country.

I get nervous when the kids start crowding around Coyote. I keep shooing the kids back, but it's hopeless. They squeal and run around to the other side. I can see all kinds of bad things happening to us once Coyote stomps a couple of their children.

But Coyote does nothing. I can't believe it. He doesn't even put his ears back. One little girl runs under his belly and all he does is look at her. If I tried that, I'd be missing something important.

Finally, I give up. I can't stop them anyway. Without me slowing them down, the kids swarm all over Coyote like ants. Small hands grab onto stirrups and saddle strings and they hoist themselves right up. In two shakes of a lamb's tail there's six of them on him, shouting and jumping around and waving their arms.

"I don't know why you're always saying your horse is so mean," Jack says.

"Because he is mean."

"Maybe you need to be nicer to him."

"Maybe you need to mind your own business."

"You're still grumpy, I can tell."

I shake my head. Why do I bother?

The villages show us to a hut. It's empty except for an old hen. She squawks angrily when they chase her out. I pull my saddle off Coyote—shaking loose a dozen little kids first—and toss my gear into the hut.

As the sun goes down it's clear they're planning a big fiesta. Kids run off into the trees and come back carrying wood. The animal they were cleaning when we got here gets put on a spit and hung over a fire. The women make some kind of dough that they form into little balls and cook in the coals.

There's also a big pot hanging over its own fire. It's thick and it looks like there's corn in it, but I can't tell what it is. Unlike the other foods, this is being cooked by the men, which makes me think it's not food at all. They keep dipping their fingers in it and laughing. Definitely not food.

It's dark when the food is ready. The meat is like nothing I've had before, stringy and lean. But it's not too bad. The little rolls and the squash are good too.

But the corn stuff in the pot? It's terrible. I choke the first time and almost spit it out. That makes all the men laugh like they never saw anything so funny. Of course, Jack has no problem with it. He smacks his lips like it's the finest whiskey ever. How does he do it? I wonder. He has a way of fitting in wherever he goes. I have to admit—only to myself naturally—that I kind of envy him for it. I mostly feel like I don't fit anywhere.

Jack was right about the card tricks too. After chow, he hunkers down next to the fire and pulls out a deck of cards. I'd forgotten how he can make them fly. I spent a lot of time practicing back when I still hoped he'd come back to the stronghold, and I'm no slouch with a deck, but I'm not within a bowshot of him. He makes cards disappear from one hand and appear in another. He makes the whole deck fly from one hand to the other.

The children stare at him with big eyes. Jack pulls a card from behind the ear of one little boy, and the boy keeps checking there afterwards to see if there are more. It's not only the children, either. Everyone is fascinated by him. They all gather around him. They seem to forget I'm even there.

I walk off into the darkness and find a spot to sit down and think. How did I end up here? How am I going to get home? I look north. Somewhere that way is home. I can't even imagine how far away it is. I wish I could mount up and ride there.

I head back to the party after a bit. I haven't been there long when the chief starts stroking my duster again. He motions that I should take it off and let him wear it. I don't see the harm in that, so I oblige him.

He puts it on and puffs up like a tom turkey, he's so proud. He takes a turn or two around the fiesta, showing it off to everyone. He doesn't come up much past my chest, so it drags on the ground, but that doesn't trouble him.

He says something to me and holds out one of his bead necklaces. I shake my head. He keeps pushing the beads at me. Finally, I take them. He walks away.

Jack comes up. "You surprised me, son," he says.

"What are you talking about?"

"Trading the chief your coat. That was a generous thing to do."

I look at the beads in my hand and feel sick. I love that coat. "All I did was let him wear it for a bit."

He laughs. "Is that what you think?"

"Oh, damn. He's not going to give it back, is he?"

"It was the right thing to do. Look at what they're doing for us."

"Why don't you give him your coat, then?"

"He doesn't want my coat. He wants yours."

"Great. I didn't even want to do this and now I lost my coat."

He claps me on the back. "You'll get over it."

Something else occurs to me. "Why'd you say you were surprised?"

"Now, don't take this wrong, but sometimes you can get a little selfish."

"What? Why would you say that? I'm not selfish!"

"You're getting upset." His breath smells like the corn brew. "I should have said fussy."

"And that's better? Fussy makes me sound like a little old lady."

"There's a saying. 'If the shoe fits, wear it.'"

"That's a dumb saying. If a shoe fits, why wouldn't you wear it?" I ask.

"The important thing is that you're starting to lighten up a little. Did you have some of that *tesguin*?"

"If you mean that corn stuff, only a little. It's horrible."

"You get used to it."

"Can't say I want to."

"You're coming along, you know that? I'd like to think I'm finally starting to rub off on you. Life's too short to worry about the little things."

"What's that supposed to be? Is that fatherly advice?"

"It is whatever you want it to be."

"I'd rather hear you say you're buying me a new coat."

"That's one of those little things I was talking about. You need to stop worrying about it."

"Says the man who still has his coat. It gets cold up here in the mountains."

"You're young and tough. You'll survive."

"Why don't you give me your coat?"

"You're getting upset again, I can tell."

"You didn't answer my question."

"It wouldn't fit you," he says.

"My coat doesn't fit the chief. It doesn't seem to matter to him."

"It's not your coat anymore, Ace. Let it go."

I want to push him down the mountain. I need to talk about something else. "Did you ask them how to get to Machu Picchu from here?"

"I asked the chief a little while ago. He laughed at me."

"So we're on our own?"

"No. Once he was done laughing, he said he'd send someone to show us the way in the morning."

"Why was he laughing?"

"I got no idea."

"Did you tell him why you want to go there? Does he know you're planning to steal their treasure?"

He looks around to make sure no one is listening in, even though we're talking in English. "Don't say that. It's not their treasure, anyway."

"It belonged to the Incas. They're about all that's left of them."

"That's a questionable claim, at best. Besides, they have no use for treasure anyway."

"How do you know? Did you ask them?"

"You're trying to be difficult. You're still mad about that little problem with the Colonel, aren't you?"

"*Little* problem? I think having the Peruvian army after us is more than a little problem."

"Little things, Ace. You have to let go of the little things."

"I give up. There's no point talking to you."

"That's because you know I'm right."

"I see why so many people want to shoot you," I say.

He pats me on the shoulder. "Don't worry. We'll find you another coat."

Chapter 37

In the morning, the chief shows up towing a boy behind him. The boy is tiny, probably not more than eight years old, with big eyes staring out from under a ragged patch of hair.

"Paíz take you," he says in broken Spanish.

"What?" I'm still waking up and I don't understand him at first.

"Machu Picchu. You still want to go, no?" He looks like he's trying not to laugh. There's something funny that he's not telling us.

"We still want to go," Jack says.

"Paíz take you."

"He's awful little," I say.

Paíz scowls and stands up straighter. He might not speak Spanish, but he knows he's being talked about.

"He plenty big," the chief says. "You see."

We say our goodbyes. The whole village turns out to see us go. The chief is there at the head of the line, strutting around in my duster, which is still dragging on the ground behind him. It breaks my heart to lose that coat. We've been through a lot together. I wish he wouldn't drag it around like that.

"Machu Picchu," the chief says, patting me on the shoulder. He laughs again. "Good luck." There's definitely some joke here we're not getting.

Paíz is looking impatient, moving from one foot to the other, so we cut it short and follow him up a skinny trail.

Pretty quick I figure out that Paíz means to teach us a lesson about doubting him. Not five minutes in, he's so far ahead we can't even see him anymore.

"Like chasing a jack rabbit," Jack says.

I'd answer, but I'm too busy sucking wind. There's not a lot of air this high up. And the trail runs about straight up the mountain. My legs are telling me I'll be hurting tomorrow.

151

We gasp and sweat our way to the top of a high ridge and find Paíz crouched there waiting for us. He grins at us. He's enjoying our suffering. He jumps up when we get close.

"How about we take a little break, partner?" Jack says.

Paíz grins bigger and darts away.

Jack swears. Even Coyote looks peeved. When I lean against him to catch my breath, he whacks me with this tail.

The whole morning goes like that. Over and over we gasp our way to the top of another horribly steep ridge, sure that this time we must be there, only to see yet another horribly steep ridge ahead. No sign of Machu Picchu. No sign of the top. Only more mountains in every direction.

After a while I'm sure Paíz is taking us the long way to torture us. Some of these ridges look familiar. I think we've climbed them twice already. When I tell Jack, all he does is wave at me. He can't breathe enough to speak.

And every time we get to the top of a ridge, Paíz jumps up and takes off again. I'm starting to hate this kid.

Around midday we stagger to the top of still another ridge. I sag down on my knees. I'm thinking about lying down and not moving again for the rest of the day. I don't care if the Colonel gets there first. All I want is to rest.

"What do you know?" Jack says. "We made it."

At least I think that's what he says. He's puffing so hard I can barely make sense of it. I look around. Sure enough, we're there.

What I notice first isn't the ruins. It's the flat ground. Well, not exactly flat. But after what we've been through, this looks like west Texas to me. I want to kiss it, it looks so good.

Paíz is standing over us, his arms crossed over his skinny chest. He looks like he could run all day still. He's all but laughing in our faces.

"I take it back," I say in Spanish.

He rattles off something I don't understand. He seems to be waiting for something.

"What do you want?" I ask.

He points at my head.

"He wants your hat," Jack says, laughing. Or maybe he's choking. He's still wheezing hard enough that I can't tell.

"He's not getting my hat. I already lost my coat. I'm not losing my hat."

"Since when did you start wearing a hat anyway? You didn't use to."

"I'm not talking about this."

Jack climbs up and reaches into his pocket. "Here, kid. I've got something for you." He pulls out a battered pocket watch and gives it to the boy. Paíz takes it with a puzzled look on his face. Jack shows him how to open the face. Paíz's eyes light up. He looks at Jack with a question on his face.

"It's yours. Go on. Take it."

Paíz backs away, eyes going from Jack, to me, and back. He's wondering if this is a trick. Then he turns and darts back down the way we came.

"Nice to see you being generous with your own things," I say.

"It's broken anyway," Jack says. "I don't guess he cares." He turns slowly, scanning the area. "I don't see any sign of the Colonel. Looks like we beat him here after all."

I stand up and look around. Plants have grown up thick over the ruins. Most of them I can barely see. "Where now?"

He shrugs. "We look around. Something will pop up."

He starts off. As for me, I've had enough walking for today. For a whole lot of days, actually. But when I try to mount up, Coyote jumps sideways and snaps his teeth at me.

"You're not going to start acting like that old man's donkey, are you?" I ask him.

He gives me a cross-eyed look.

"Fine. I'll walk. Miserable horse."

I figure we're not going to find anything. This was always a wild goose chase. I keep my eyes peeled for the Colonel.

Then Jack says, "This is it."

I look over at him. He's standing by this big stone, looking at it. "What are you talking about?"

He points at the stone. "This is what was drawn on the other half of the map."

The stone is covered in plants and it takes me a minute to see it, but then I do. It's been chiseled flat on the sides and the top. There's a rectangular piece sticking up from the top and what kind of looks like a big step cut into the side.

"What now?" I say.

Jack walks around it, studying it. "We're going to need the machete."

153

We bought the machete in Lima when we picked up supplies for the trip. Jack goes to get it. Coyote tilts his head to let Jack scratch him behind the ear. I'm never buying oats for that horse again.

It only takes a few minutes to clear a fair bit of the brush away. The stone looks even weirder now. Jack climbs up on the big step and crouches down to look at something.

Jack looks over his shoulder and grins at me. "I know what that strange white stone is for, the one that was in the box. It's a key."

I climb up there beside him. Sure enough, there's a hole in the rock about the right size.

"Let's see if I'm right." He pulls the white stone out of his pocket, scrapes some moss away, and pushes it into the hole.

There's a click.

"What do you know?" he says.

I've got nothing to say. I can't believe this man's luck.

He pushes on the stone. It doesn't move. "Help me," he says.

At first nothing happens, but then, with a grinding sound, the stone slides back, revealing an entrance and stairs leading down into darkness.

Chapter 38

"We did it," Jack says. He's smiling so big he's bound to crack his jaw. "We did it." He's saying it like he can't believe it and needs to convince himself.

Standing there, looking down those dark stairs, I've got a whole different feeling. All of a sudden, I'm remembering the lost temple of Totec, what it was like inside there.

How close I came to dying more than once.

Am I really going to do this again?

Jack's smile fades a little. "What is it? You look like someone just stepped on your grave."

"Whatever happens, I leave first," I tell him. "Got that?"

"What?"

I tap myself on the chest. "On the way out, I lead the way. Not you. Understand?"

"Sure. Whatever. What's got you so jumpy?"

"I'm not getting left behind again," I say.

He shakes his head. "You still have that lantern, I hope."

"I got it." I go to get the lantern off Coyote. He tries to step on my foot.

"I'm done talking to you," I tell him.

The lantern is a little one like the miners use. I was hoping we wouldn't need it.

Jack sets to lighting it. I feel sick. The thought of going underground and facing who knows what is hitting me pretty hard all of a sudden.

"You gonna be okay?" he asks, peering at me.

"I'm fine. Let's get this over with. You first."

"So you want me to go first on the way in, but you want to go first on the way out?"

"Exactly."

"What's wrong with you?"

"Nothing. I don't want to talk about it."

"Have it your way." He picks up the lantern and heads down into darkness.

I stand at the doorway and look around at the sky and the mountains. It's all bright and sunny and open. Why would anyone ever want to go underground?

"Coming?" Jack calls.

I grumble and walk through the doorway. I take two steps and stop. I suddenly feel like there isn't enough air. I swear I can feel the stone pushing down on me.

Jack is a dozen steps down. He looks back at me, wondering why I stopped.

"You claustrophobic?" he asks.

"I don't know what that is."

"Afraid of tight spaces. Like this."

"What kind of fool wouldn't be? This could all fall down and crush us at any second."

He shrugs. "Point taken. Come on. Quit dawdling. We don't want to be down here when the Colonel shows up."

That gets me going. The only thing worse than being trapped underground is being trapped underground with a bunch of soldiers shooting at you. I know this from personal experience.

The stairs end after a couple of minutes. We're standing in a cavern. I can't tell how big it is. The light from the lantern doesn't reach far enough.

"Would you look at that? This feller has been here for a while," Jack says, pointing at a skeleton lying on the ground. He looks at me. "What's got you so skittish?"

I've got one of my pistols out and I'm pointing it at the skeleton. I didn't even realize I'd drawn it.

"It's dead already, Ace."

"That doesn't mean it'll stay dead."

"That sounds *loco*. You know that, right?"

"You weren't there on the old Spanish ship. Some skeletons don't stay dead." I nudge it with the toe of my boot, ready to start shooting if it moves. But all it does is break up into pieces. I put my gun away.

"Once we get out of here, I have got to hear more of your stories. You've lived some interesting times, it sounds like."

"Interesting is one word for it. Not the one I'd choose." The skeleton is wearing some bits of rag and boots that are little more than scraps of leather. Lying beside it is an ancient black powder pistol, the likes of which I've never seen before, along with a sword that's mostly rust. Jack is right. This fellow has been here a long time.

"I reckon he came down here looking for the treasure and got trapped," Jack says. "Poor fool."

"Or his partners left him behind. They betrayed him when he didn't expect it."

Jack looks at me curiously, then shakes his head and walks off, holding the lantern up. I kick the sword and the pistol out of the skeleton's reach and follow him.

We don't see anything until we get to the far side of the cavern. There's a large stone door set into the wall. It has a big, nasty face carved into it, all sharp teeth and glaring eyes. It's not Xipe Totec, but it sure doesn't look friendly.

Jack reaches out to touch it.

"Don't go touching it!" I snap, jumping back.

"What's gotten into you, Ace? You're jumpier than a snake in a chicken coop."

"You shouldn't just go touching things. Stuff like that is dangerous. You touch the wrong part and you're dead."

"It's a stone. The only way it's going to kill you is if it falls on you."

"That's what you think. Until the walls close in and try to crush you."

"What walls?" he says, looking around.

"So there's no walls. There's lots of other terrible things that can happen."

He frowns at me. "You feel all right?"

"I'm fine. I don't want to get killed is all. Let's find your damned Heart of the Empire and get out of here." I'm feeling more tense by the minute. Any minute now something's bound to come out of the darkness and attack us. The Colonel and his men are sure to show up about the same time. I squint into the darkness. "We should have brought more lanterns."

He shakes his head and turns to look at the door again. "I wonder how you open it."

"Some parts of it move. You push them and it opens. But if you push them in the wrong order, something bad happens."

"Where do you get these crazy ideas?" he asks.

"I think we should pull out. We'll hide and wait for the Colonel. Let him get himself killed opening that, then we'll come back and pick up the ruby." That's what I say out loud. What I'm thinking is that if I get out of this hole in the ground, I'm never setting foot in it again. I'm done.

"That's a rotten idea. I'm not letting the Colonel get the treasure. I came too far, went through too much to get here."

Why did I know he would say that?

"How about I go back up top and keep a watch for the Colonel?" I say.

He's not listening. He leans close, studying the door. "What do you know? This tooth here looks like it moves." He reaches for it.

I holler and try to stop him, but I'm too late.

The piece slides inward. There's a rumbling sound. Little rocks fall from the ceiling.

"What did I tell you?" I yell. "I told you not to touch it. Now you went and killed us both."

"You need to calm down. Nobody's getting killed. See?" He spreads his arms.

I look around. No walls closing in. No dead gods coming to life. Maybe I *am* a touch jumpy.

Jack pushes on the door, but it doesn't open. "There must be another one," he says. He holds his lantern up and looks closely at the carving.

After a few minutes, he steps back. "I don't see anything." He cracks his knuckles. "Time for Lady Luck to pay us a visit."

He sets his lantern down. He closes his eyes and puts his hands on the carving. Murmuring something under his breath, he moves his hands over the carving like a blind man.

"That's not going to work," I say. "It's time to go." I turn to look at the stairs. Still no sign of the Colonel, but I know he's going to pop up any second.

"Come on," Jack says. "Papa needs a new pair of shoes."

I start to ask him what he means by that, but right then he pushes on both eyes at the same time.

The door swings open silently.

Chapter 39

Jack turns to me. "You ready for this, cowboy?" I've never seen anyone look so excited. He's practically jumping up and down.

I don't feel the same way. I feel like a chicken on the block, waiting for the axe to fall.

"Let's get this over with."

He frowns. "What made you this way?"

I check them off on my fingers. "Almost getting killed in the temple of Totec. Being attacked by skeletons in the belly of a wrecked Spanish galleon. A man trying to feed me to the sharks to steal the black pearls. I have more if you want them."

He rolls his eyes. "That's enough. Forget I asked."

He goes through the doorway. I turn around and eyeball the room. No sign of the Colonel yet. Or ancient gods.

It's only a matter of time.

I take a deep breath and follow him.

We go into a room carved out of solid rock. The walls of the room are covered with carvings, hundreds of them, everything from geometric shapes to snakes and bizarre, winged creatures. In the middle of the room, sitting on a large block of white stone, is an ancient, wooden chest. Instead of hinges, it has leather straps that have rotted away to nothing. Set into the lid is a black gem. Jack stands there, staring down at it, his eyes bright like he has a fever.

"What are you waiting for?" I ask him.

"Hold your horses," he says. "I'm trying to savor the moment. I've waited a long time for this, you know."

"Can't you savor it outside?"

"It wouldn't be the same." He holds out his hands. They're shaking slightly. Which surprises me. He has the steadiest hands I've ever seen. "Look at me. I'm shaking like a ten-cent bride on her wedding night."

"Ten-cent bride? Do people buy their wives?"

"It's a saying."

"Not one I've ever heard."

"There's lots you never heard. Now be quiet and let me enjoy this."

Gently, he takes hold of the lid. He lifts it and sets it aside. His smile disappears.

"No," he says, his voice cracked.

I look into the chest. It's empty.

"Looks like someone got here before us," I say.

Then he does something I don't expect.

He starts laughing.

I'm confused. "Why are you laughing?"

"What else am I supposed to do? Cry?"

"Some would."

He leans against the side of the chest. His laughing sounds an awful lot like crying now. Not sure what else to do, I pat him on the back.

"It's okay," I say.

"Sure, it is. I spent years of my life chasing a ruby that someone already got. To do that I pissed off the most dangerous man in Peru. I also owe way too much money to a man who feeds his enemies to piranhas. Everything's peachy."

"Maybe it's time to hop a ship and sail back to America."

"Not much else I can do, is there?" He looks back into the chest. "I just figured it out."

"What?"

"I know why the chief was laughing at us. He knew all along the ruby was gone." He swears softly.

"I shouldn't have let him take my coat," I say.

Jack turns away from the empty chest. "Let's get out of here."

We turn around to leave. Standing in the doorway is the Colonel.

Why am I not surprised?

Chapter 40

"Leaving so soon? But you only got here," the Colonel says. Beside him is the sergeant, pointing a pistol at us. The Colonel comes into the room, soldiers following.

"We've decided to get out of the treasure business," I say. "There's nothing in it."

The sergeant comes forward and barks at his men to disarm us.

"The ruby is gone," Jack says. "Someone beat us to it. By about a hundred years, I'd say."

"You gentlemen give up too easily," the Colonel says.

"Weren't you listening?" Jack says. "There's nothing here. We'll be going now."

He starts for the door. A couple of rifle barrels pressed into his chest stop him in his tracks.

"You're not going to get fussy and blame us for this, are you?" Jack asks. "We're victims here too."

"I'm disappointed," the Colonel says. "I did not think you would surrender so easily, Jack."

Jack scratches his head. "What part of, 'it's gone' doesn't make sense to you?"

"Clearly you have not done your research. If you did, you would know that this room is a false front," the Colonel says. "It was meant to deceive thieves if they ever made it this far. The Incas often concealed their treasures in another chamber behind the first one." He looks around the room. "I am certain there is another door here somewhere."

"Good luck finding it," Jack says.

"In this, I will not need luck." The Colonel gestures. Two soldiers enter the room carrying sledgehammers.

"They say the only thing better than luck is a large hammer," Jack says.

"Or two," I say.

"I have not heard this saying," the Colonel says.

"Probably because he just made it up," I say. "He does that."

The soldiers begin swinging. Stone crumbles. Dust fills the air. I catch Jack's eye, thinking now would be a good time to make a break for it. As if reading my mind, the sergeant waggles his gun and shakes his head. That man is a little too sharp for my tastes. I prefer the brainless underlings.

One of the hammers hits with a different sound. The soldier steps back. There's a neat round hole in the wall.

"I believe we have found it," the Colonel says.

Chapter 41

Soon the whole doorway is exposed. The Colonel motions and his men shove us toward it. "Does this mean you want us to go first?" I ask. Jack is already headed for the door. I grab his shoulder. "You know there's going to be something bad in there, don't you?"

He pulls away. "I don't care."

"If you do not go, my men will shoot you down right here," the Colonel says. "That should make your decision easier."

Jack goes through the doorway. I look at all the guns pointed at me and decide to follow him. The Colonel is right. It is an easy decision.

The passage I find myself in is more of a crack than a tunnel. It's narrow and low. It leads down and around some sharp bends. Then it opens up into a cavern.

Cutting across the cavern is a wide chasm. On the other side of the chasm, on a narrow ledge, is a stone statue of a bestial creature with glaring eyes and long, curved fangs. Sitting in the mouth of the creature is the Heart of the Empire.

The Heart is the deep red of heart's blood and as big as both my fists together. It sits in a pool of light, as if a shaft of sunlight is somehow making its way down from aboveground. Or maybe the light comes from inside it. It's the most stunning thing I've ever seen.

We all stop—Jack, me, the Colonel, the soldiers—and stare at it, openmouthed. No one moves. No one speaks for a long minute. We can only stare in awe. The ruby demands that.

Jack breaks the spell first.

"It's beautiful. It's..." He can't find any more words.

"It is the heart of a new empire," the Colonel says, reaching for it with one gloved hand, as if he could take it from where he stands.

We move closer. Hushed whispers come from the soldiers. The whispers sound like prayers. I see some crossing themselves. I'm not the only one who doesn't want to be here.

The chasm is about thirty feet wide. It's spanned by an ancient rope bridge that looks like it will collapse at the first touch. I can't see the bottom of the chasm. The edge is unstable. Some small stones come loose and fall. It takes way too long for them to hit bottom. I move back. One wrong step here would be my last.

The Colonel points at me. "Go. Get the stone."

"No," Jack says. "I'll go."

The Colonel swings toward him, surprised. "This is not like you, Jack, to volunteer yourself for danger when another could risk it. Why this sudden change, I wonder?"

Jack realizes then that the Colonel hasn't figured out I'm his son. He tries to cover for it. "I want to get my hands on it, even if it's only for a minute. I've come too far."

"No, that's not it," the Colonel says. He looks at me. "Who are you? I know of you. I know that you arrived only days ago on a ship from San Francisco, the mysterious man with the ugly horse."

I open my mouth to defend Coyote, then shut it again. It's probably not that important right now.

"Right away you took up with Jack. On the docks, you defended him against those who were angered by his cheating. Why? What is your stake in this?"

"He's no one," Jack says. "I needed someone who was good with a gun, so I hired him."

"There are many in Peru who are good with guns. Why bring someone all the way from America?" The Colonel's gaze is intense. This is a man who is used to figuring things out.

"I needed someone I could trust. We worked together before," Jack says.

The Colonel taps his chin with a long finger. "He is too young. You have been in Peru for several years, Jack. He would have been little more than a child when you were last in America."

"I'm older than I look," I say. I don't like being talked about like I'm not there.

"It's because he can't grow a beard," Jack says. "That's what makes him look so young. They call him the Babyface Kid back home."

I give him a look. The Babyface Kid? If we survive this, I'm going to make him pay for that one.

The Colonel isn't convinced. He looks from me, to Jack, then back to me. All at once he figures it out. "This is your son."

"That's crazy," Jack says. "How could he be my son? He's Apache. We don't even look alike."

The Colonel is smiling. "It is in his eyes. How did I miss it? It is so clear now."

"My name is Ace, not the Babyface Kid." I feel it's important to clear that up. I don't need that moniker following me around.

"So he's my son," Jack says. "What difference does it make? I'll go get the ruby."

"It makes all the difference. Now I don't have to worry about whether you will behave or not. You are a man who would gamble with his own life, Jack, but you will not gamble with the life of your son."

"That shows what you know," I say, but he ignores me.

"I'm done talking about this." Jack turns for the bridge.

The Colonel motions. The sergeant grabs Jack and drags him back. When Jack resists, he clubs him over the ear with the butt of his gun. Jack sags to his knees. He looks up at the Colonel. Blood is running down the side of his neck.

"We have a rope," Jack says. "You can send one of your men to get it off the horse. At least let me tie a rope to him."

"No."

"The bridge is rotten," Jack says, his voice rising. For the first time since we've been together his calm cracks. He looks badly rattled. More than that, he looks afraid. "It'll never hold. You know that."

"I do not know that," the Colonel replies. "Neither do you. It *looks* like it will not hold. Certainly, I would not gamble my life on it. But looks often deceive and even the unexpected card can make an appearance in the game. Sometimes it is even an ace." He winks at me as he says the last part.

Jack staggers to his feet. He's swaying badly. The sergeant raises his pistol to club him again, but the Colonel shakes his head.

"Do not interfere, Jack."

"There's no reason to do this!"

"But there is. There is the thrill of it. Come, Jack. Surely you can understand. Once again we play a game with the highest stakes."

"Damnit! Not everything is a game!"

"That's where you're wrong. There are games within games. This, right here, is one game, but it is only part of a larger game. With this ruby in my possession, I can throw the dice in a much larger game." He looks very pleased with himself. He's practically rubbing his hands together.

"What game is that?" I ask.

"It does not concern you."

"I think it does. I'm about to risk my life for it."

He thinks about this, then nods. "Fair enough. It is a game for the whole of South America. Your father thinks my goal is to conquer Chile. But Chile is nothing! Why stop there? Why should Peru not conquer all of South America, the way America will soon conquer all of North America? Why should Peru not become a world power the equal of anything Europe has to offer? This ruby, and the price it will fetch, will buy the soldiers and the guns necessary to make this happen."

"What's President Menendez going to say when he learns what you're doing?" I say.

"It will not matter. He will not be president for long." He makes a fist. "Soon it will be me. But I will not settle for the lowly title of president. Once before this land was the heart of an empire, the Inca Empire. Now it will be the heart of a new empire, and I will be its emperor."

"That's quite a jump, from colonel to emperor," I say.

"Only by taking the greatest risks can the greatest prize be won," he says. "Now, go." He draws his pistol and points it at Jack. "Or I will shoot your father."

Why did I know it would come to this? From the first moment I laid eyes on the treasure map, I knew I would end up in some dark place risking my life for it. I wish I was even a little bit surprised.

"There's no need for that," I say. "I'll do it."

I have to pass by Jack on my way to the bridge. He grabs my arm and pulls me close. He looks into my eyes. "I'm sorry, Ace.

I'm sorry I got you into this. I was wrong. I'll make it up to you, you'll see."

Strangely, I believe him. I heard it in his voice when he tried to get the Colonel to let him cross the bridge. I see it in his eyes now. For once he actually is sorry about what he's done.

But I have the vague workings of a plan cooking in the back of my mind. If I want it to work, I need to play it up now.

I jerk my arm away and shove him hard. He almost falls. "Save it," I growl. "This is all your fault. If I survive this, I'm going to kill you."

He kind of crumples when I say this, like a horse kicked him in the stomach. I feel bad for it. But there's not time for that right now. I turn away and walk to the end of the bridge.

There are four ropes to the bridge, two for holding onto, two more supporting the wooden slats for walking on. Up close the bridge looks even worse than I thought. The ropes are badly frayed and gray with age. The wooden slats are riddled with cracks.

It's not a matter of *if* this bridge collapses, it's *when* it collapses.

Gripping the side ropes, I step out onto the bridge…

Which immediately drops—

Chapter 42

My heart leaps into my throat. I brace against the impact.

But I don't fall, or only for about a foot. The bridge groans but doesn't break.

"That was thrilling, wasn't it?" the Colonel says. He sounds excited. "I thought it was going to be over before it started. My heart is still racing. What about you, Jack?"

"I'm going to shoot you in the face," Jack snaps.

"Far more likely that I shoot you," the Colonel replies. He says it like he's thinking of having another piece of chicken for dinner, instead of killing a man. "Don't stop now!" he calls out to me.

This is crazy. I'll never make it across. But I don't have any choice. I'm not sure I ever did.

I take another step.

The slat breaks immediately. My foot plunges through and only my hold on the side ropes keeps me from following the wood splinters down into the abyss. I hang there, breathing hard.

"It's very old wood," the Colonel says. "You should expect some breakage."

I pull myself back up. "Why don't you come out here and show me how to do it."

"Not on your life," the Colonel says and chuckles like he just made the world's greatest joke. "Jack, would you like to place a side wager on whether he makes it or not? I will give you substantial odds." Jack doesn't answer.

The next few slats are in better shape. I keep to the edges and none of them break. I'm about halfway across and feeling a little better now. Maybe I'm going to survive this after all.

The next slat crumbles to powder almost the instant I touch it. Once again, I fall. But I'm ready for it. I've got good holds on both sides.

What I'm not ready for is for is the rope in my left hand to break.

168

"Are you okay?" Jack calls out.

That seems like a foolish question to me. I'm not dead, which counts for a lot. But I'm swinging there in mid-air, holding on with only my right hand, a thousand feet of nothing under my boots, so I'm a long way from okay.

I grab on with my left hand and pull myself back up. I still have the slats and one side rope to hold onto, but things are lot wobblier now. The bridge is swinging side to side. The remaining three ropes are creaking, this close to breaking.

It's time to get off this thing. I plot the remaining distance. I should be able to cover it in four long steps.

I take the next step. Right away I feel the slat giving away, but this time I keep going. As the slat falls away, I'm already putting my weight on the next one.

It cracks too, but I don't slow down. I'm practically running by now.

One more step, another broken slat, and then I simply jump.

The bridge sags badly when I do that, taking most of the oomph out of my jump. I go down short of the far end, the last few slats shattering as I hit them.

I reach for the rocky edge, manage to get my hands on it, but there's nothing to get hold of.

I'm going down.

Chapter 43

The next couple of moments are real bad. I claw wildly at the edge of the chasm, trying to find even a tiny crack I can get a fingernail into.

At the last moment I find one and manage to stop my fall. I dangle there, my heart pounding hard. That was way too close.

"He did it!" the Colonel says. "That was most impressive. You should have taken the bet, Jack. I thought for sure he wasn't going to make it."

Grunting, I pull myself up and roll onto the ledge. He's not the only one who thought I wasn't going to make it.

"Congratulations," the Colonel calls over to me. "You made it. Now get the ruby."

I walk over to the statue. It's a little taller than I am and a lot wider. It's carved out of black, volcanic rock. The body of the creature is kind of a mix of a snake and a lion, and it has wings, ugly, stubby things spread wide. Its mouth gapes wide, long teeth curving down past its jaw.

The ruby sits on its tongue. Up close it's even more impressive. I don't care much for shiny rocks, but this one is something to see all right. It catches the light in dozens of places, winking at me as I move closer.

I hesitate before reaching for the ruby. Why does it have to be in the monster's mouth? I ask myself. Why couldn't it be lying on the ground or something? I just know that mouth is going to slam shut once I touch the ruby. I don't want to go around with only one hand for the rest of my life.

"Don't falter now," the Colonel says. "You've come so far."

I start to reach with my right hand, then change my mind and reach with my left. If I have to lose one of them, I'd rather it was the left.

I pluck the stone from the mouth and jump back.

Nothing.

The carved creature doesn't come to life. Nothing jumps out and attacks me. The ceiling doesn't collapse.

It must be broken.

I head back to the bridge, then stop at the edge.

"Good, very good," the Colonel says. "Now throw it here."

I shake my head. "I don't think so. Once I throw you the stone, what's to stop you from shooting me or cutting the bridge and leaving me here?"

The Colonel nods like he expected this. He points his pistol at Jack's head. "Throw it, or I shoot him. You have five seconds."

Instead I hold the ruby out over the chasm. "You do that, and I'll throw it in."

"You're bluffing," he says. "You'd never risk your father's life."

"Try me," I say, casually flipping the stone into the air. It spins, reaches the top of its flight, then falls back down. I snatch it one-handed. When I look over at the Colonel, I can see that he is rattled, though he quickly hides it.

"You thought I was going to drop it, didn't you?" I say.

"I had every confidence you would catch it. Why throw away your only card? But enough of this. Throw me the stone, or I will shoot your father." He cocks the pistol.

I toss the stone again, higher this time. I hear someone suck in a breath. I'm willing to bet it was the Colonel.

"Go ahead," I say. "He's not my father. He's a liar and a thief, is what he is. He tricked me into coming to Peru, and he tricked me into chasing this treasure. I've risked my life because of him. Go ahead and shoot him. You'll be doing me a favor."

"You don't mean that."

"Are you sure?"

"You rescued him from me. You wouldn't do that if you didn't care about him."

"I rescued him because of the treasure. I knew I couldn't find it without him. Without the treasure, I have no way out of this crappy country. That's all it was."

"You don't mean that." He shoves the barrel against Jack's head.

"Shoot him and find out." I flip the stone into the air again. This time I bobble the catch on purpose. For a moment it looks like I'm going to drop it.

171

When I look at the Colonel again, he's a little pale and I know I've won this round. There's one thing at least he's not ready to gamble with.

He motions and the soldiers point their guns at me. "Maybe I will have them shoot you down instead."

"You could do that. But I'm standing awful close to the edge. I'll probably fall in when I die. Along with this pretty rock."

He lowers the pistol. "What do you want?" he says.

"All I want is to survive. That's not so much, is it?"

He points at Jack. "He stole from me. I cannot let this pass. He must pay the price."

"I don't care what you do to him," I say. "It's me I'm worried about. I want to get out of this hole and ride away. I'll get on a ship and you'll never see me again."

He ponders this, then nods. "It is a deal. You have my word on it."

"Your word isn't worth a buzzard's gizzard," I say. "I need something more."

"Like what?"

"Give your gun to Jack."

"So that he can shoot me? That would be a foolish thing to do." While he's talking, he lowers his gun and holds it down by his leg.

"Now why would he do that? So your men could shoot us down right after? He's a liar and a thief, but he's no fool. He knows the best we can manage is what they call a Mexican standoff. No one shoots because no one wants to die."

"And then you will throw the stone over?"

"No. Then I will carry the stone over to you."

"And what if you fall?"

"That is the risk you must take, Colonel." I smile real big at him. "What kind of a game is it without the thrill?"

"If you have some plan to cheat me, I will make sure you die slowly."

I shake off his threat. "I'm sure it will be terrible. Look, I'm not going to try and cheat you. I don't care about this rock. I only want to get out of here alive and say goodbye to this country forever."

"Okay. As you wish." He hands the pistol over to Jack, who points it at him. I can see how badly he wants to shoot the Colonel.

I tuck the ruby inside my shirt. It's too big for my pocket.

Then I take hold of the bridge and start the trip back. I'm not even trying to step on the slats this time. They're worse than useless. I hold onto the remaining upper rope and plant my feet directly on the rope below it. It's wobbly as hell, but I can make it.

As long as the ropes don't break.

"Be careful," the Colonel hisses.

That's something he doesn't need to tell me. Now that I'm out here, I'm wondering why I didn't demand he throw me a rope. That would have been the smart thing to do.

I hope I live long enough to learn my lesson.

I'm about halfway across and starting to think I might survive this after all, when there's a couple of snapping sounds. Suddenly I'm falling through open air...

Chapter 44

Lucky for me the ropes broke behind me. I'm swinging fast for the side of the cliff. Pain shoots through my knee as I slam into the rock. My hold on the rope slips, but I've got a death grip on it and no way am I letting go.

Faces appear above me. Jack calls out, "Hold on! I'll pull you up."

"Don't," I say. This rope is too fragile. If he goes dragging it over the lip of the chasm, it's going to break again for sure.

I start shimmying up the rope. There's a small ledge about ten feet from the top. I pause there to flex my hands and catch my breath. Then I climb up the rest of the way.

Soon I'm standing on solid ground once again. Well, not that solid. I feel the edge start to give under me and I have to take a quick step forward.

The Colonel is standing well back from the chasm, his soldiers spread out on both sides of him. Jack is right in front of me.

"You made it," he says.

I give him a look and walk past him and over to the Colonel.

"A deal is a deal," I say, pulling the ruby out of my shirt and handing it to him. "I honored my side."

He takes it and stares greedily at it. He looks at me. "And I will honor my side. You are free to leave."

Suddenly he snatches a pistol from one of the soldiers and raises it. I duck, thinking he's going to shoot me. He fires.

I stand up, surprised that he could have missed at such short range.

I hear a grunt of pain from behind me and turn. Jack is standing there at the edge of the chasm, looking down at the bullet hole in his shoulder.

"You shot me, you bastard," he says. He raises his gun and points it at the Colonel, who doesn't so much as blink an eye.

Jack squeezes the trigger.

Click.

The Colonel's smile gets wider. "You didn't think I'd really give you a loaded gun, did you?"

Jack opens his mouth to reply—

But then the edge gives way under him and with a small cry he falls backward into the chasm.

For a heartbeat, I can only stare at the spot where he was standing. I can't believe he's dead. It doesn't seem possible.

Then a howl comes from my throat. It doesn't sound like anything a human could make. It is an animal sound, the sound of a wild creature driven berserk.

I throw myself at the Colonel. He tries to bring his gun around, but I knock it from his hand. It hits the ground and spins away.

I lock one hand around his throat and squeeze with all my strength. With the other hand I smash him in the face. Blood bursts from his nose and his lip. I keep hitting him as hard and as fast as I can. I want him to die. I want to beat him to death. Soldiers crowd around, hitting me, but I can barely feel it.

My next blow drives him to his knees. He's bleeding hard now. He tries to crawl away, but I break free of the soldiers' clutches and kick him in the ribs, once, twice.

On the second kick the ruby flies out of his hand and bounces away toward the chasm.

With a wail, he crawls after it on his hands and knees. But I don't let up. I follow, kicking him again and again.

He almost gets hold of the ruby again, but his hand is slippery with blood and it slips out of his grasp. It slides over to the edge of the chasm.

I barely notice the ruby. I'm intent on making this bastard pay for killing my father. I throw myself at him again.

But finally, there are too many soldiers. I can't get loose no matter how I try.

The Colonel crawls over to the ruby. His hand closes on it. He stands up and turns around. His smile is bloody and triumphant. His eyes are wild.

"It is mine!" he shouts. "I will be emperor!"

There's a sudden cracking sound and the edge crumbles under him. He manages to grab hold of the edge and stop himself, but his hold is precarious.

175

"Help me!" he yells.

None of the soldiers run to help him. They all stand there staring at him.

The edge gives way and he is gone.

Chapter 45

For a moment no one moves. The soldiers mutter between themselves. It is obvious they had no love for the man. They let me go.

I run for the chasm and look over the edge, wild thoughts of getting a rope and climbing down. Maybe my father is still alive down there.

What I see is my father about ten feet down, holding onto one of the bridge ropes, standing on the narrow ledge.

He grins. "Are you going to stand there and stare at me, or are you going to help me up?"

"You're...alive." I'm still having a hard time believing it.

"Not for long if you don't do something. I expect this ledge is going to give way any second. Low quality rock they have around here."

I flop down on my stomach, take hold of the rope with both hands, and begin pulling him up. I can feel how close the ancient rope is to breaking. I pray it holds a tiny bit longer. I only need another foot or so.

A foot turns into inches. Then he is in reach.

The rope breaks, but at the same moment I lunge and grab his hand. He yells as the jolt hurts his wounded shoulder. I'm not sure how I manage it, but somehow I'm able to pull him up and over the edge.

We both lie there, breathing hard. Then he starts laughing.

"That was something, wasn't it?"

"I thought you were dead."

"So did I. Good thing you left that rope there for me."

"I thought you might need it."

"I can't believe it."

"Can't believe what??"

"That I didn't notice that he'd emptied the gun. I should have figured he'd cheat. I guess I'm slipping, getting old. You look like hell, by the way."

I touch my face. It feels puffy and hurts everywhere. I guess the soldiers landed a few. "At least I don't have any bullet holes in me."

He winces. "It smarts." He peers at it. "I think it went through though. Give me something to tie around it and I'll be all right."

I tear some strips from my shirt, and we make a bandage that will hold for now. I stand up and help him to his feet.

"Sorry about your treasure, Pa," I say.

"Oh, well. Easy come, easy go, as they say."

I snort. "You call that easy?"

Then his mouth drops open. "You just called me Pa."

I think about this. "So I did."

"Well…that's great, Ace. It's really great."

"You finally acted like one."

That strikes him. "I did, didn't I?"

"Think you can keep it up?"

He nods slowly. "I can sure try."

He looks unsure, so I add, "Maybe I shouldn't bet on it, though, right?"

"Make sure you get some good odds anyway."

As we head for the exit, I realize a few of the soldiers are still standing around. The sergeant is one of them. They have their guns in their hands, but they can't quite seem to figure out if they should point them at us or not.

"What are you still doing here?" I ask them.

The sergeant scratches his chin. "I don't know."

"Are you planning on shooting us?"

"I don't know."

"What are you going to tell your superiors?"

He looks pained. "I don't know."

"There's not much you do know, is there?"

"No."

"Are you going to help us?"

This one he knows. "No."

"I think we all need to go home," Jack says.

The sergeant nods. "*Sí.*" He motions to the others. They put their guns away and file out of the cavern.

Chapter 46

The rough bandage helps, but Pa is still bleeding from his shoulder. My knee, where I slammed it into the cliff, is swollen and so stiff I can barely bend it. My face hurts pretty bad from the pounding I took, and one eye is swollen partway closed. It takes us awhile to limp across the outer cavern. The soldiers are long gone by the time we reach the stairs leading out.

We make our way up the stairs, taking our time. I'm tired. It feels like all the running I've been doing ever since I got to Peru is catching up with me all at once. I'd like to lie down and sleep for at least a week.

There's a surprise waiting for us outside.

We step out into the sunlight and there's Myron and Lonnie. They look pretty scratched up. Myron's shirt is nothing but rags. I guess they made their escape during the confusion when I rescued my father. It looks like they threw themselves down the side of the mountain.

They're pointing guns at us.

"Where is it?" Myron says. He's got dried blood on the side of his face and leaves stuck in his hair. He lost his floppy hat and his face is burned bright red.

Jack and I look at them and start laughing.

"What are you laughing at? This isn't funny."

But it is funny. After all we've been through, they just don't seem important.

We don't even slow down. We walk right on by them.

"We'll shoot you," Lonnie squawks. His hat looks like a bull stomped it. Half of the brim is torn off.

"Go ahead. Already been shot once today," Jack says.

"We're not playing around here!" Lonnie says.

"Neither are we. We're done playing for today," Jack says.

Myron lowers his gun first. "Let 'em go."

"But he cheated us!"

179

"Hell, we ain't got no bullets anyhow, and it's clear they ain't got no treasure."

"He's right," I tell Lonnie. "There was a giant ruby, but the Colonel got it."

"Where's he at?" Lonnie asks, craning his neck to look past us, like maybe we're hiding him or something. "Them soldiers came out and rode away, but we didn't see him anywhere."

"He's with the ruby. Down at the bottom of a deep hole."

"Damnation!" Lonnie yells suddenly. He throws his pistol down and then kicks it for good measure. "All we went through and we get nothing!"

"You're richer for the experience," Jack says with a straight face.

"Richer for the...? What in tarnation is that supposed to mean?"

"It means you learned an important life lesson."

"I don't wanna learn no damned life lesson. I want my treasure."

"Can't help you there," Jack says. "Maybe it's time to start looking for the next treasure. I heard there's this Spanish ship loaded with gold that went down off—"

Lonnie stuffs his fingers in his ears. "I ain't listening! I cain't hear what you say!"

"A ship loaded with gold?" Myron says, his ears perking up.

"What the hell's wrong with you?" Lonnie yells at him. "Don't listen to him. Didn't you learn anything?"

"Oh, yeah, right. He'd only cheat us again, wouldn't he?"

"You think, Myron?" Lonnie says sarcastically.

"I...I do. Don't I?" Myron is now good and confused.

Lonnie turns a dark look on my father. "I ought to shoot you just for leaving us with the Colonel."

"I gave you a chance to escape in the confusion. What more do you want?" Jack asks. "Besides, you look like you came out of it all right."

"We fell halfway down the mountain getting away!" Lonnie cries. "And we were still tied up. We had the devil's own time getting the ropes off. Getting back onto the road wasn't no picnic neither."

"Look at the bright side. You built a lot of character in the last few days."

"What the hell do I want with character? You can't eat it, can you? Can't buy whiskey with it. I got all the character I need."

"And that's why you're never going to get anywhere, Lonnie," Jack says. "You lack vision. That's your problem."

"No, my problem is you." Lonnie picks up his gun and points it at Jack again.

"It's empty, remember?" Jack says.

"I could still throw it at you."

"You could. But you might lose it. Best to hang onto it, don't you think?"

"He's got a point there, Lonnie," Myron says.

"Don't take his side! I'm your brother, you durn fool. We hate him, remember?"

"Yeah." Myron hangs his head. "I kinda forgot, is all."

"You'd forget where your head was if I wasn't here to remind you."

"That ain't nice, Lonnie. Remember what Mama said about being nice."

"Well, Mama ain't here, is she?" Lonnie turns back to us. "I won't forget this, Jack. I'm going to hunt you down and—"

"Get some bullets first."

"What?"

"Before you hunt me down, you ought to lay in some lead. It'll go easier that way."

He frowns. "Of course, I'm going to get more bullets first. What do you think I am, an idiot?"

He starts ranting and raving. He's so angry he can't see straight. Myron pats him on the back, which only makes him angrier.

"Let's get out of here," Jack says. "Somewhere there's a soft bed calling my name."

Chapter 47

We're riding down out of the mountains. We should make it back to Lima by the end of the day. Now that we're getting close, there's some things that need resolving. I have questions I've been wanting to ask ever since Machu Picchu

"What are you going to do?" I ask Jack. "When we get back to Lima?"

"I'm going to figure a way to get you onto a ship back to America, is what I'm going to do," he says. He's been quiet a lot these last few days. He's been doing a lot of thinking from what I can see. "I don't know how yet, but I've got a couple of ideas. One of them will pan out."

"I'm not talking about that. You missed El Chacal's deadline. You don't have the money to pay him. Shouldn't you be thinking about getting yourself on a boat too?"

"Probably," he admits. "But I hate the thought of letting him run me out of town. I'll go when I feel like going, you know?"

"That's purely foolish. Did you forget about his fish? Is that how you want to end up?"

He does that thing with his hand. But this time I'm not going to stand for it.

"No. Not this time, you don't."

"Don't what? What are you talking about?"

"That thing you do, where you wave something off like it's nothing. You don't get to do that this time. That man will kill you. That's a real problem."

He gives me a tired smile. His wound is healing pretty good, but I can see it's taking a lot out of him. Fortunately, we were able to get him a horse. We found the Colonel's horse following Coyote around.

"It's *my* problem, not yours," he says.

"The way I see it, it's our problem."

"No, it's not." He scratches his goatee. "I realized something back there, when you were crossing the bridge."

"What's that?"

"I've been letting other people take the fall for me my whole life. I finally saw the truth of that. I thought you were going to die. And if you did, it was *my* fault. Mine. No one else's. I'm not going to do that anymore. When I do something stupid, I'm the one who's going to pay the price. No one else."

"I notice you said 'when' and not 'if.'"

His old grin comes back. "Some things aren't going to change. I'm not ready to curl up and die just yet."

"Well, if you're not leaving, then I'm not. I'm staying until we get this tussle with El Chacal sorted out."

"I swear to God, but you can be a stubborn one sometimes. You're as bad as your mother."

"Stubborn just means I don't give up easy. How do you think my clan survived in the mountains all these years? We know how to hang on. We also know how to look out for each other."

He opens his mouth to speak and closes it again. A few seconds pass. Then he starts blinking real fast. At first, I think he has something in his eye. Then I realize those are tears. He brushes them away.

"Dammit, Ace." His voice is rough. "What did you have to go and do that for?"

I look away to give him a chance to gather himself.

"Family sticks together," I say. "Isn't that what it's about?"

"I reckon you're right. Kinda forgot that somewhere along the way." He's quiet for a bit, then says, "I wonder how my ma is doing. I haven't seen her in a coon's age."

That surprises me. For some reason I never thought about my family on that side. "What's she like? Where does she live?"

"You'd like her. She's a tough old bird. She lives in Missouri. Last I checked, anyway. She was always saying it was getting too civilized and threatening to move west. As far as I know, she could be in Oregon by now. No one tells her she can't do something."

"What about your father?"

He shrugs. "Never met him. Ma never talked about him unless she was swearing. A no-account drifter from what she says."

That gives me something to think about. I have a grandmother and maybe a grandfather out there somewhere. I wonder if I'll ever meet either of them.

"Back to your question, Ace."

"Which one?"

"About why I don't drag my freight and leave town. It's not really about not wanting to let El Chacal run me out of town. There's a bigger reason why I can't leave yet."

"What's that?"

"Because I have unfinished business. A new well."

I don't know what he's talking about at first. "A new well?"

"I told Olivia I was going to get Barrio Mariposa a new well dug."

"I forgot about that."

"Hell, it's the least I can do after the way those folks took me to heart. You saw how they are. They're good people. I can't run on them. That's what I've done my whole life. When I told Olivia I'd get them a new well, I don't think I really meant it. It just sounded good. But now I can see it's something I got to do. I don't expect you to understand."

"But I do."

"You do?"

"I sold a handful of black pearls a while back. Sold isn't really the right word. There was this nasty business involving sharks and drowning. Anyway, I spent most of the money on supplies to take back to the stronghold."

"Yep. You see now why I won't go."

"I do. And I mean to help."

"It's not your yoke."

"It is now." I've got some ideas starting to bubble up. "The way I see it, we have two problems here. One is El Chacal. He wants to kill you for not paying him his money. The other is the well you promised that can't get dug without money. I think we can solve them both at the same time."

"I'm not following you. Where are you going with this?"

I grin at him. "We're going to rob El Chacal."

Chapter 48

"Rob El Chacal? Are you serious?"

"As serious as a skunk with a sore tooth."

He stares at me, then shakes his head. "I don't know whether you're plumb *loco* or bold as hell."

"Sound like anyone you know?"

He grins. "You take after your old man more than I realized." He thinks about it, then says, "The brothers go out every morning in a coach to collect the earnings from his businesses around the city. We could just rob that."

I shake my head. "You're thinking too small. If we're going to hit El Chacal, let's make it hurt. Let's cripple him."

He nods and a slow smile builds on his face. "Are you saying what I think you're saying?"

"Let's take *all* his money. He's run over the people of Lima long enough, don't you think?"

"He keeps his money in a safe in his office. I've seen it."

A safe. Of course, he does. With a sick feeling in my gut, I ask, "It's not a Hammerstein, is it?"

He gives me an odd look. "It is. How did you know that?"

"I didn't. It was an unlucky guess. Don't people buy any other kind?"

"Not if they want to keep their valuables safe. They make the best safes—"

"In the world. Yeah, I know that."

"We'll need dynamite to get it open."

I remember the safe at General de la Cruz's hacienda. I shake my head. "Nope. We're definitely not doing dynamite."

"You sure?"

"I'm sure. It's tricky. Either you don't use enough dynamite, in which case the safe doesn't crack and you made enough noise to bring everyone in the whole city running. Or you use too much and what's left isn't worth scraping up."

He looks at me in a new way. "It sounds like you have some experience here."

"More than I'd like."

"There's some stories there, I think."

"Let's say that me and dynamite and safes have a long, painful history. We need to hit him when the safe is already open."

"It's risky. When that safe's open he always has a passel of hired guns around."

"Since when did a little risk start to worry you?"

"Since…oh, the hell with it. Here I am trying to be a good, upstanding father, and you're the one roping me into a hare-brained scheme. I give up. I'm in. Let's do this."

"All we need to do is be there when he opens the safe. He probably opens it every day, doesn't he? Putting in what he's earned, paying out what needs paying."

"Sure, we'll waltz in there and take it. No problem."

"We're going to need some help. Can you manage that?"

"No problem. I'll talk to Olivia. She'll get us some people from the *barrio*."

"It's risky. Are you sure you want to bring them in on this?"

"We'll tell them your plan. Let them decide. What is your plan anyway?"

"I'm still working it out. I don't know enough yet." I tell him what I've come up with so far. His eyes get wide.

"Holy smokes, Ace. That's a bold plan. There's about a hundred ways it could go sideways. Are you sure you want to do this? This isn't your fight."

"I don't like people like El Chacal, bullies who prey on the weak. Something about them gets stuck in my craw. They need to be taken down."

He pushes his hat back. "You look a little scary right now, you know?"

"So, what do you think? Are you in?"

"I was always in." He sticks out his hand. I shake it. "Jack and Ace on the same side. How can we lose?" he says.

"We could get shot. Or stabbed. The brothers could snap us in half like twigs."

He waves this off with that little gesture of his. "After what we've been through? That's nothing."

"Let's go find Olivia."

We enter Lima cautiously, keeping our heads down and our hats pulled low. I tuck my hair up under my hat, knowing it makes me stand out a bit.

We stay off Jack's usual routes and make our way to Barrio Mariposa. Word spreads and young boys run on ahead of us as we ride down the narrow streets. Old men nod from shadowed doorways. Señoritas smile and turn their faces away.

Olivia is waiting in the plaza, her hands on her hips.

"They didn't get you."

Jack swings down. "Not this time. Did you have trouble after we were gone?"

"No trouble. The Colonel was too busy chasing you. You were all he could see. After this dies down…?" She shrugs. The shrug reminds me of my mother. She does that same thing. There's a whole world of meaning in that movement. It means what is to come will come. It means there's no getting around it, only through it. It is the shrug of someone who has endured much and is still not broken.

Jack grins at her. "You don't have to worry about the Colonel. Ever again."

She raises an eyebrow. "Did he get lost in the mountains?"

"Something like that. Wasn't looking where he was going and fell over a cliff."

A smile twitches her lips. "And the treasure?"

"You know about the treasure?" Jack asks.

She pats him on the shoulder. "Everybody knows about the treasure, Jack. Lima is not so big. Word gets around."

He looks at me. "How do you like that? And here I thought I was keeping it all under my hat." He turns back to Olivia. "The Colonel took it with him."

Another shrug. She doesn't seem bothered by this at all. "Treasure comes with curses," she says.

I agree with her there. Nothing good comes from chasing treasure.

"Why are you here?" she asks. "El Chacal will know to look here. He has too many eyes."

"That's why we're here. We have a plan for El Chacal, but we need help. If it goes right, he won't be a problem anymore either."

187

Now she gets a real big smile on her face. The Colonel was a problem, but mostly a distant one. El Chacal is like ants in the flour, always there, stinging and stealing. "What is your plan?"

Chapter 49

It's the next morning. Jack and I are standing in the alley beside a tall wooden building. I'm wearing a tattered, filthy old dress. It goes clear to the ground, covering my feet. I've got a scarf wrapped around my head. The women rubbed ash into my hair so now it looks gray. I'm carrying a woven basket over one arm. If you don't look too close, I could pass for one of the hundreds of peasant women who dot the streets of the city. At least for a few seconds. And that's all we need.

"Here it comes," Jack says.

This isn't the same coach the brothers picked us up in before. That one was all about fancy and soft. This one is about protecting El Chacal's money.

It's solidly built and wrapped in iron bands. It looks like it could take a dynamite blast or two. There are bars in the windows. On the driver's seat are two men, both wearing long, black coats and black hats. One drives, the other holds a shotgun. They look like men doing the same job they've done hundreds of times before with no trouble. No one is stupid enough to steal from El Chacal.

The coach comes to a stop in front of the building. The driver sets the brake. He takes a shotgun from under the seat and he and the other guard jump down. They take up positions flanking the front door of the building, shotguns at the ready.

The coach doors open. The coach creaks and settles to one side as first Chato, then Gordo, climb out. They're bigger than I remember, built like brick shithouses, as the saying goes, though why someone would waste good bricks building a place to poop is beyond me.

Both brothers are wearing pistols, but they look small and kind of useless against their bulk. I get the feeling these boys prefer settling problems with muscle rather than lead. I think I'd rather be shot than have one of them get his hands on me.

Chato and Gordo enter the building.

"Time to go," Jack says.

I head out into the street. I wobble as I walk, trying my best to look like a harmless old woman. I keep my head down so they can't see my face. From the edge of my vision I see the guard nearest me glance my way. But he only sees an old peasant woman and his eyes move on, tracking other people moving on the street. Most of them are helping us. The group of boys kicking a rock around down the street. The old woman sweeping the walkway in front of a house. The young woman selling flowers from a basket. They're all from the barrio.

"Please help," I say when I get close. I'm trying to make my voice sound like an old woman's. I think it sounds pretty close. I sure got a lot of laughs last night while I was practicing.

"Move along, *vieja*," the guard growls.

"It's my baby," I moan. "I think he's sick. I'm afraid. Please help me." As I say this, I'm pulling off the cloth covering the basket.

"I don't care about your baby. Get out of here," he says.

"But you haven't looked at him," I cry shoving the basket at him. "He isn't moving."

With the cloth moved, the smell comes out strong. It hits him hard. He glances into the basket. His face twists up when he sees what's inside.

"God, that's disgusting! What is that? Get it away from me."

It is disgusting. It's not a baby, but a dead dog. A very dead dog. The boys found it at the city dump last night. I told them the rottener the better. They took me at my word.

He pushes the basket away. When he does, I pretend like I lose hold of it.

It tips over. The dead dog slides out in a wave of tangled guts and collected juices. It splashes onto him in a sticky, wet mass.

"Aaugh!" he cries. "You got it on my pants! What's wrong with you?"

He takes a step back, brushing at the front of his pants. There's bits of dead dog everywhere. It's horrible.

That's when I act.

I swing the basket at his head. Hidden in the bottom are two sizable rocks. It hits him like a hammer. His eyes roll back in his head and he goes to his knees.

Meanwhile, Jack goes into action. While I was distracting the guards, he was sneaking up on them from behind. The second guard is starting to bring his shotgun around when Jack clubs him over the ear with the butt of his pistol. He drops like a wet rag.

The people from the barrio drop what they were doing and converge on us. The people in the street who aren't involved quickly avert their eyes and decide they have somewhere else to be. They scurry away without looking back. No one wants to see anything.

The guard I hit is still on his knees, so I whack him again with the basket. He pitches onto his face.

Now we have to hurry. We have only a couple of minutes at most before the brothers come back out with the money.

I strip off the dress and scarf I'm wearing and toss them aside. I roll the guard over and start peeling off his black coat. Two of the young women who were selling flowers help me. We get him out of it pretty quick. I put it on and one of them hands me his hat. The other hands me his shotgun.

Jack has been doing the same thing with the other guard. His moans and tries to fight back a little. The old woman kicks him and spits on him.

"For shame," she hisses. "You used to be a good boy. What happened to you?"

Once we have them stripped, our helpers take hold of them and drag them away to the alley. Two of them are carrying ropes. I asked last night what they were going to do with the guards.

"They'll be taken out of the city and thrown on the dump," Olivia said. "If they know what's good for them, they won't come back."

Jack and I take up our positions on either side of the doorway. I tuck my hair under the guard's hat and pull it down low. People hurry back to their places.

None too soon, either. About then the door opens. The brothers come out. Chato has a small cloth bag in his hand. We're turned partly away, looking like we're scanning the street for trouble, but they don't so much as glance at us. They climb into the coach and close the door behind them. Everything is working perfect so far.

So why am I suddenly as skittish as a colt that smells a cougar? I can't put my finger on it, but something feels wrong.

Too late now, though. As Jack would say, the dice are down. Nothing to do now but wait and see what turns up.

We climb up onto the stage. Jack takes the reins. He gives me a grin.

"Hot damn. It's going down just like we planned," he says.

"Something's not right. I can feel it in my gut."

"Probably all those chiles you ate last night," he says, slapping me on the back. "I told you not to eat so many."

I don't think that's it, but I let it go. Jack snaps the reins and the coach starts rolling.

Chapter 50

We deliberately hit them at their last stop, figuring the fewer chances they had to look at us the better. We head for El Chacal's hacienda. I check the loads on my guns one more time.

At the hacienda, the guards open the gate and wave us through without paying us much mind. This is something they do every day. They're used to it. Besides, who would be crazy enough to tangle with the most powerful man in the city? That's why they don't pay any attention to us.

At least, that's what I keep telling myself. Like saying it often enough will make it true. But when those gates clang shut behind us, I feel like the coyote does when the jaws of the trap close on his leg.

We rumble on into the main courtyard. There are men with rifles standing around. Are there more of them than the last time I was here? Or am I imagining it? I wipe the sweat off my hands and try to look bored. Nothing to see here, folks. Only another hired gun doing his job.

We're coming up on another dangerous spot. Thanks to the information we gathered from people in the barrio, we knew a lot about what Chato and Gordo do on their cash runs. What we don't know is much, or anything, really, about what happens once the coach gets back to the hacienda. We're going to have to wing it from here on out.

Jack sets the brake. The brothers climb out and head for the main building. We hop down and follow.

Every step I'm waiting for the brothers to turn on us. Or for someone to start shouting. But neither of those things happens. It's all going smooth. I need to calm down.

I'll calm down once I'm on a ship headed back north.

We pass by the archway that leads to the smaller courtyard where Chacal keeps his toothy fish. I shudder a little. Those things scare me. Maybe we could toss a stick of dynamite in there before we leave. We brought some with us just in case. Jack has it tucked inside his shirt.

The front doors are huge and sheathed in brightly-polished brass. A servant opens the doors. We follow the brothers inside.

The room we walk into is huge, bigger than a lot of barns I've been in. Light comes in through an archway at the rear. There's a fireplace big enough to cook a whole steer in, heavy chairs arranged in a half circle in front of it. On the wall is a massive painting of El Chacal wearing a white suit, a rifle over his shoulder. A maid in a black and white uniform is dusting a shelf filled with stone statues. A stairway curves upward to the second floor.

When I see the stairway, all I can think is *Please, not up there.*

So, of course, that's where we go. Our boots are terribly loud on the stairs, the sounds echoing through the silence. Now I'm sure the brothers are going to turn on us. What reason could there possibly be for the guards to follow them up here? We're in the heart of El Chacal's kingdom.

But the brothers plod forward without hesitation. I wipe sweat from my forehead with the back of my hand. It feels very hot in here.

At the top of the stairs we turn down a dim hallway. There are closed doors on both sides. From behind one I hear a woman laugh. In the distance a dog barks.

We keep passing doors. How long is this hallway? Is this a trap? I'm glad I checked the ammo in this shotgun I'm carrying. I'd hate to find out it's actually empty.

The hallways ends in a door. One of the brothers pushes it open.

We walk into El Chacal's office. Two tall windows let in light. The shelves are covered with books that have never been opened. El Chacal wants to look smart.

El Chacal is sitting behind a desk that's big enough to double as a dance floor. He's wearing his usual white suit and writing on a piece of paper. In the corner of the room is his safe. The door is open. The piles of cash in there are enough to take a man's breath away. It seems stealing from the people of Lima is good business. I want to shoot him right now.

Jack and I stop just inside the door. The brothers walk forward and set the sacks on El Chacal's desk. He looks up. Then he notices us for the first time and looks our way.

"What are you doing here?"

Jack pushes his hat back. "We've come to make a withdrawal, El Chacal." We point the shotguns at the three of them and cock them.

The brothers don't so much as blink. They stare at us stone-faced. We are only stray dogs in the street to them.

El Chacal sits back in his chair and steeples his hands. "You're both dead men. I'm talking to dead men."

"We're holding the guns," I say, waving my shotgun a little to make sure he notices. "You see them, right?"

"All I see are two dead men who haven't figured out they're dead yet."

"We'll see about that," Jack says. "Are you going to hand the money over easy, or do we get to splash your body parts around the room? I know which one I'm hoping for."

"It's money you want? Is that all this is? By all means, help yourselves. Take as much as you can carry out of here." He gestures toward the safe. "Maybe we could find you some sacks to help you carry it all."

"We're not playing with you, El Chacal," Jack says, shouldering the shotgun. "I will shoot you."

"You'd never leave this place," he says calmly. "It would be better to keep me alive and use me as a hostage."

I glance at Jack. We talked about that.

El Chacal takes a cigar from a box on his desk and holds it up to the light. "I assume you have a ship ready to sail?" He looks from one to the other. "No? Surely you know there is nowhere in Lima, in all of Peru, where you will be safe after this."

"Yeah, we got a ship."

Which isn't true. But that's the future. Right now I'm focused on surviving the next five minutes.

I still have a sinking feeling this is a trap. El Chacal is too calm. He didn't look surprised to see us at all.

But we're holding the shotguns. If shooting starts, it's going to get messy in here. Most likely Chacal will end up with a face full of lead.

So why does he look so calm? He's almost eager.

Then I feel a gun barrel press into my back.

Chapter 51

From the corner of my eye, I see a gun pressed to Jack's back too.

They were standing behind the door.

Stupid, stupid, stupid. I should have looked.

I'll give Jack credit. He doesn't so much as flinch. He keeps the shotgun fixed on El Chacal. "I can still kill you," he says. "I can rid this city of its biggest rat."

"You'll be dead too," El Chacal points out.

"I'm dead either way," Jack says. "But if I go down killing you, I call that a win."

"And your son? You've gotten him killed too. What about that?" El Chacal leans forward.

"He knew the risks coming in."

I feel like I should add something. "I'm going to shoot you too. Make sure you're really dead. You can never tell with rats."

"That *does* sound bad," El Chacal says, leaning back once again. "Even if I survive, I imagine I will be terribly wounded."

Then he smiles. There's a whole lot of darkness there.

"There is one thing I want to tell you. There's someone else here, someone you might know."

He nods and someone limps into the room.

It's Pedro, Olivia's grandson, the boy who wants to be a gunfighter. At first, I think he's a hostage, that El Chacal is going to use him against us. But something doesn't look right. Pedro doesn't look scared. Mostly he looks…

Guilty.

He betrayed us.

"You see it now, don't you?" El Chacal says. His eyes are flashing. "This is a young man who knows how to back a winning horse. A young man who is going places."

"Pedro, why?" Jack says. Pedro won't look at us. He stands with his head down, staring at his feet.

"He came here early this morning and told me everything," El Chacal says. He puts his hands behind his head and leans back, chuckling a little. "He told me all about your foolish plan. So I prepared this little surprise for you both."

Jack hisses and squeezes the trigger on his shotgun.

Click.

"They're loaded with dummies," El Chacal says.

Jack drops the shotgun. His hand moves toward his gun.

"One more inch, and I'll have my man kill you on the spot," Chacal says. "You'll never even touch your gun."

I drop my shotgun too. No sense in holding onto it now. Hands relieve me of my pistols. I sure do seem to get them taken away a lot lately. But then, that's not going to be a problem in a few minutes. Not once I'm dead.

"Do it. Shoot us now and be done with it," Jack says.

I look at him in surprise. Getting shot isn't something I want to rush into.

"For one thing, the rug you are standing on was brought at great cost from Morocco. I would hate to have it stained with blood and guts." El Chacal stands. "For another, my little friends are very hungry. They haven't eaten yet today."

Oh, shit. He's going to feed us to those damned fish. This plan is looking stupider by the second. I should have left the country when I had the chance.

Chapter 52

Chato clamps a hand the size of a large steak on the back of my neck. Gordo grabs hold of Jack. They half carry us down the stairs.

I try to come up with a way to escape, but nothing comes to mind. It's hard to do much when someone is carrying you by the scruff of the neck like a kitten.

I really don't want to be eaten by a fish. I already saw that up close with the sharks. Which is worse? I wonder. A thousand tiny bites, or a couple of huge ones?

El Chacal follows us out to the small courtyard. The brothers haul us over near the pool and plop us down. Chato switches his grip to my arms.

"I knew you would never come up with the money," El Chacal says to my father. "You're the type of weasel who never does. I almost killed you the last time I had you here."

"Then why didn't you?" Jack's trying to come up with a plan. I can see it in his eyes. It doesn't look like he's having any more luck than I am.

So far I've got nothing. I've got no guns. A man the size of an ox has his hands clamped on my arms. I couldn't break his grip with a sledgehammer. I'm like a fawn facing a wolf.

We're going to need a miracle.

"I didn't kill you then because I knew about the map you'd stolen from the Colonel." Jack gives him a look. "Don't look so surprised," El Chacal says. "You should know by now nothing happens in this city that I don't know about."

Is there anyone in Lima who didn't know about the map?

A servant walks up with a silver tray and sets it on the small table by the pool. It looks like the same old woman who served El Chacal the last time we were here. On the tray is a silver coffee pot and a cup. With her is another servant, a young girl. She is carrying a plate with several pieces of raw meat on it. El Chacal picks up one of the pieces of meat and tosses it into the pool. The water foams madly as the piranhas swarm it. I feel sick.

"I like to get them excited first," El Chacal explains. "Get a real frenzy going before I toss them their prey."

He takes the coffee cup and holds it out for the old woman to fill. He takes a sip and sighs. "Hot enough to remove skin. Just the way I like it." He takes another sip and puts the cup back on the tray.

"I had real hopes that you would recover the treasure," he says. "You're slippery enough that I thought you might pull it off. Then I would get back the money you owed me, along with substantial interest." He smiles. "What am I saying? I would have taken all of it."

"I'm sorry to disappoint you," Jack says.

"This is almost better," El Chacal says. "As you saw, I have plenty of money. It's entertainment, true entertainment, that I find hard to come by." He flashes his teeth at us. "The kind of entertainment that comes from watching my enemies scream their lives out as my little friends eat them."

"You can keep waiting. I'm not screaming," Jack says.

I wish I could say the same.

"Yes, you will," El Chacal says. "You'll scream and scream. They always do. Before you die, I want to thank you for something. You did me a favor, getting rid of the Colonel. He had been making noises about moving against me. I would have beaten him, but this way is cleaner, no waste of men or gold."

"I'm glad we could be of help," Jack says.

"I don't want to wait any longer. It is time for my entertainment," El Chacal says. He looks at Chato. "Throw the son in first. You can watch your son die before you do, Jack."

As he's speaking, I feel Chato's hands loosen a tiny bit as he prepares to shift his grip so he can throw me in the pool. It's the opening I've been waiting for.

I twist free of his grasp and spin toward him. I haul off and kick him in the knee as hard as I can.

Nothing. His face shows no expression at all. What's he made out of, wood?

I follow that up with a couples of jabs to his face, throwing everything I have into the blows.

Ouch. Forget wood. I think he's made out of stone.

200

At least he reacts this time. He smiles.

I swing again.

Chato grabs my fist in mid-air. My hand disappears in his huge mitt. He bends my wrist back. With a grunt of pain, I go to my knees. It's either that or get my wrist broken.

His other hand comes down and lands on my shoulder. He squeezes tight enough that I can feel the bones grinding together. I have to grit my teeth against the pain.

Everything turns upside down as he jerks me into the air and holds me with both hands over his head. He takes a step closer to the pool.

And I see my miracle.

Like all miracles, it comes from where it's least expected. And it's brought by an angel.

The servant woman—old, gray-haired, all of five feet tall and probably eighty-five pounds—snatches the coffee pot off the tray and throws the coffee in Chato's face.

Chato screams, his voice oddly high-pitched. He drops me and puts his hands to his face.

I fall halfway in the pool. Instantly I can feel the piranhas swarming around my legs. Sharp pains as several of them bite through my trousers, taking chunks of flesh.

But I'm not staying around for this. I'm already turning as I hit the water. I once saw a cowboy try to throw a cat in a wash tub. That's me, claws out, getting away from that water whatever it takes.

I come flying out of the water. The servant woman holds out the coffee pot. I grab it and turn. Chato is bent over, holding his face. I club him on the side of the head with it. There's a hollow ringing sound and he falls back a step.

Everyone else is reacting by now.

The other servant, the young girl? She's got this little silver knife in her hand. She buries it in Gordo's back.

Gordo roars, lets go of Jack, and reaches for the girl with one hand. With his other hand he's trying to get hold of the knife and pull it out. She darts between his legs. Somehow he gets tangled up in her and falls down.

Shouts and running feet on the other side of the archway as some of El Chacal's hired thugs come running, drawn by the shouts. We've only got a few seconds at best.

I hit Chato again with the coffee pot as he comes for me—it's dented all out of shape now—but it doesn't do much this time. He grabs me in a bear hug and picks me up. His face is blistered from the coffee and his eyes are squeezed shut, but he doesn't need to see for this. He squeezes and I feel a couple of ribs crack. Sparks of pain fly across my vision.

I don't waste my time trying to pull free. I'd have better luck removing a bear trap with both hands tied behind my back. Speaking of hands, mine are pinned by my sides. I can barely move them. I try a couple of head butts, but they only seem to make Chato squeeze harder.

But I feel something with the fingers of my left hand.

It's the butt of Chato's pistol.

I fumble for it. Another rib cracks. I manage to get the pistol free, then almost drop it. The pain is incredible. I feel like someone dropped a mountain on me.

My finger finds the trigger.

The first shot goes through his foot. Chato grunts, but it's not enough to convince him to drop me.

I work the barrel around before shooting again. I expect this one will get his attention a little better.

The next shot hits him in the groin. That gets a response.

He screams. He sounds like a little girl. I must have blown off something valuable.

He lets go and staggers backward, hands clamped to his crotch. There's a whole lot of blood. His pants are half soaked already.

I shoot him in the chest, and he goes down.

I turn. Gordo has his thick hands wrapped around Jack's neck. Jack's face is a surprising shade of purple already.

I shoot Gordo twice. He doesn't seem to notice. I shoot him twice more. Finally, I hit something important. He goes limp, collapsing across Jack.

Breathing hard, I turn and point the gun at Chacal. He's standing by the pool, a short-barreled pistol in his hand. Standing next to him is Pedro, watching everything with his mouth open.

"Your gun is empty now!" El Chacal shouts. "Time to die!"

I tense to throw myself at him, even though I know I'm too far away. He'll shoot me at least once, probably twice, before I can get to him. Jack's trapped under Gordo. There's nothing he can do. The first wave of thugs is running into the courtyard.

And now another miracle, another angel.

Pedro looks up. El Chacal is still screaming. He's not paying any attention to the boy.

Pedro shoves El Chacal.

For a moment El Chacal balances on the edge of the pool, his mouth wide, his eyes disbelieving.

Then he topples backward. He manages to get one hand on the boy as he goes, but I haven't been standing around doing nothing. I grab Pedro's hand and yank him away.

El Chacal falls into the pool.

The water churns madly, like a pot at full boil. El Chacal rises partway out of the water, screaming. He's got fish hanging off his face, his neck, his arms.

He goes back under. The water turns red.

One hand comes out of the water and grabs the edge of the pool. While I'm trying to decide whether to kick it back in or pull him out, his face surfaces one last time. One whole cheek is gone. Both eyes are gone. His lips are in tatters.

He tries to say something, then slips back down into the water and is gone.

Chapter 53

Pedro looks at me. There are tears running down his face.

"I'm sorry," he says. "He say he hurt my grandmother. She is the only family I have left."

"It's okay. I understand."

El Chacal dropped his pistol when he fell in the pool. Trying not to look at the scraps in the water that used to be a person, I pick it up and turn around. There are seven of his hired guns in the courtyard now. They're just standing there. They saw what happened to their boss. The man who paid them is dead.

But they're all holding guns. There's no way to tell what they might do. I hold the pistol ready, not quite pointing at them, but close.

"What's it going to be?" I say. "I might not kill all of you, but I'm sure enough going to kill six of you. Or, we could all just walk away. What do you say?"

One of them mutters angrily and lifts his gun. I turn my gun, fire, and drop him.

"We know what he chose," I say. "Who's next?"

The fight goes out of them all at once. One of them argues with the others, but they ignore him. Guns are holstered and they begin turning away. I guess money and fear don't buy as much loyalty as they used to.

I breathe a little easier. We might still get out of here in one piece.

Jack is still trying to get Gordo off him. With the help of Pedro, the young girl and the old woman, we finally manage to roll Gordo over. Jack gets up and dusts himself off.

"I like how you took a nap and let us do all the heavy lifting," I say.

"Like trying to move a dead bull," he complains. He looks me over. "You okay?"

I take a painful breath. "It hurts, but I'll live." I turn to our three angels. "If it wasn't for you, though…"

The old lady gives me a toothless grin. "Olivia is my niece. I heard what you were planning."

Jack shakes his head. "Is there anyone in this city who didn't know our plan?"

"I knew," the little girl pipes up. She spits on Gordo's body. "I hate these pigs."

Pedro looks miserable. Jack pats him on the shoulder. "Don't worry about it," he says. "I saw what you did. It was very brave."

"You think?" Pedro says.

"Tonight, at the fiesta, you three are the heroes," Jack says. "I'll make sure everyone knows." He looks at me. "We better get up to El Chacal's office and get that money before his thugs start to get bright ideas and there's nothing left."

We head into the house. The servants and hired guns are already stealing everything they can carry. Paintings, silver, crystal, even furniture. So ends El Chacal's little empire. There won't be much left but a shell come morning.

None of them have gotten into the office yet. We go in and close the door.

Chapter 54

We stand in the office and look at the money in the safe.

"That's a lot of money," Jack says finally. "A lot more than they'll need to dig a new well."

I look at him, wondering. How much is he going to take for himself? A man could live the rest of his life comfortably on what is in that safe. Even after paying for a well.

What he says next surprises me.

"There are five barrios in Lima. I think we should divide it up between them. What do you think?"

I'm stunned. I'm no longer sure I know this man at all. A few days ago, I was sure the only one he thought about was himself, and now this? "It's a great idea. Most of it belongs to those folks anyway," I say. "Do you know who to turn the money over to in those barrios, or you just going to throw a sack on the ground as we ride through?"

"Olivia will know who to give it to." He walks over to the safe and picks up a bundle of bills. "It's going to be a lot to carry on horseback."

"We don't need to. We've got a coach. It's already set up for carrying money too. I bet the horses are still hitched to it."

He thumbs through the bundle of bills he's holding, giving it a quick count, then hands it to me. "This should be enough to get you on a ship heading north."

"Coyote too?"

"Him too."

We load the cash into the coach. Pedro and the two servants climb in and we drive to Barrio Mariposa. Olivia's eyes get real big when she sees all the money. She about hugs the stuffing out of both of us. That sets my ribs to hurting something fierce, but it's all right. I'll heal. And it still beats getting eaten by piranhas.

We spend the rest of the day driving the coach around Lima to the other barrios. At each one Olivia meets with one or two people and hands over a sack of cash. It isn't long before we have a whole parade of people of all ages following the coach. They sing and dance and really raise a ruckus, which brings people out of their shops and homes to see what is happening. I have to admit, it makes me a bit uneasy.

"We're drawing a lot of notice here. Aren't you worried the law is going to stick their noses in to see what the fuss is all about?" I'm picturing ending up in jail, the money confiscated.

Jack makes that waving off motion. "I wouldn't fret about it, son," he says. "Between them, the Colonel and El Chacal pretty much ran this city. With both of them gone, I don't think anyone really knows who's in charge."

"What about the president?"

"He doesn't leave his compound much. He's too afraid of being assassinated by some power-hungry officer in the army."

"And what about those officers? Don't they want to get their hands on it too?"

"With the Colonel gone, I expect they're busy hunting each other down. In a few days or a few weeks one of them will rise to the top, but there won't be anything they can do then."

That eases my worries some. I turn and look back. The parade is three or four blocks long now. A couple of people have horns and one man is carrying a guitar. The noise gets louder. Jack sees me looking back and turns to look too.

"I think there's going to be a big fiesta in Lima tonight." There's a slot in the back of the seat that lets the driver of the coach talk to the passengers. He slides it open and leans close.

"Hey, Olivia. What say we make a couple of stops on the way back to Mariposa and pick up some grub for a party tonight?"

Her smiling face appears at the opening. That tells us all we need to know.

The fiesta ends up lasting all night long and from what I hear later most of the city got involved. I can't rightly say one way or the other. For me the night is a blur of people pounding me on the back and passing me bottles and cups to drink from. In the end I need a couple of days before I feel like myself again.

A few days later word comes that there's a ship sailing for Los Angeles leaving with the tide. I say a lot of teary goodbyes. Jack and I saddle up and head down to the docks.

Coyote figures out right away what's about to happen. He lays his ears back and gets grumpier than a goat with a chipped horn. He tries to bite me twice after I get off.

"Knock it off," I tell him. "You really want to walk the whole way back to the States? You have any idea how far that is?" He doesn't. But then, I don't either. I only know we sailed for a lot of days getting here.

Coyote's answer is to try and step on my foot, but I'm too quick for him.

"Enough!" I whack him on the nose. "If you want to be mad at someone, be mad at him." I jerk my thumb at Jack. "He's the one who dragged us into this."

Coyote gives Jack a yellow look.

"He's right," Jack says, scratching Coyote behind the ear. "Don't blame him. It was my fault."

I wait for him to get bitten or kicked. When Coyote is in a mood, no one is safe around him. But instead he kind of sighs and puts his chin on Jack's shoulder.

"What?" I yell at him. "You lousy traitor!"

Jack laughs. "Maybe you should try scratching him behind the ears once in a while."

"And get my finger bitten off?"

Jack takes Coyote by the nose. "You take care of him, okay? He's young and reckless."

Coyote snorts. I don't think I like his tone.

"Are you sure you won't come?" I ask Jack. It's not the first time I've asked. I've gotten to like him over the last few days. I never saw that coming.

"No. I'm going to stick around here for a bit. I want to help out."

"You mean, work?"

He laughs. "I can work."

"Sure, you can." The captain of the ship yells over that it's time to load up. "Look me up when you get back," I tell Jack.

He gives me a hug. I'm surprised at first. Then I hug him back.

"I'll do that," he says. "In the meantime, I'll keep my eye on the newspapers. I have a feeling you're not done with your adventures just yet."

THE SECRETS OF MACHU PICCHU

THE END

ABOUT THE AUTHOR

Born in 1965, I grew up on a working cattle ranch in the desert thirty miles from Wickenburg, Arizona, which at that time was exactly the middle of nowhere. Work, cactus and heat were plentiful, forms of recreation were not. The TV got two channels when it wanted to, and only in the evening after someone hand cranked the balky diesel generator to life. All of which meant that my primary form of escape was reading.

At 18 I escaped to Tucson where I attended the University of Arizona. A number of fruitless attempts at productive majors followed, none of which stuck. Discovering I liked writing, I tried journalism two separate times, but had to drop it when I realized that I had no intention of conducting interviews with actual people but preferred simply making them up.

After graduating with a degree in Creative Writing in 1989, I backpacked Europe with a friend and caught the travel bug. With no meaningful job prospects, I hitchhiked around the U.S. for a while then went back to school to learn to be a high school English teacher. I got a teaching job right out of school in the middle of the year. The job lasted exactly one semester, or until I received my summer pay and realized I actually had money to continue backpacking.

The next stop was Australia, where I hoped to spend six months, working wherever I could, then a few months in New Zealand and the South Pacific Islands. However, my plans changed irrevocably when I met a lovely Swiss woman, Claudia, in Alice Springs. Undoubtedly swept away by my lack of a job or real future, she agreed to allow me to follow her back to Switzerland where, a few months later, she gave up her job to continue traveling with me. Over the next couple years we backpacked the U.S., Eastern Europe and Australia/New Zealand, before marrying and settling in the mountains of Colorado, in a small town called Salida.

In Colorado, after starving for a couple of years, we started our own electronics business, because electronics seemed a logical career choice for someone with a Creative Writing degree.

Around the turn of the century we had a couple of sons, Dylan and Daniel (I say 'we', but when the hard part of having kids came around, there was remarkably little for me to do). Those boys, much to my surprise, have grown up to be amazingly awesome people, doubtless due to their mother's steadying influence during their formative years, and not to the endless stream of bad jokes and puns spewing from their father.

In 2005 we shut the business down and moved back to Tucson. I am currently writing full time.

Made in the USA
Columbia, SC
14 April 2020

92040917R00129